My love!

Charles M. Toller

SEPTEMBER
28
2020

HIDDEN SECRETS

OF A

MARRIED MAN

CHARLES M. TOLBERT

ISBN- 978-1-09831-948-9 (print)
ISBN- 978-1-09831-949-6 (ebook)

Cover design by: 99Designs
Library of Congress Control Number: 2018675309
Printed in the United States of America

ABOUT THE AUTHOR...

While sitting in midst of darkness, captive of inability to reach the sky of potentials, I've discovered light in the 21st century as a writer, by bringing life through a pen and paper, tapping into a world of imagination, a movie coming right out of a book. As I began to write, I asked myself the very question, why would someone want to read my book? The more I asked that question, the more it became clear... People like to read suspense, mystery, and drama!

So, in this book, not only that I give that to the readers, I also invite them into the book, as though they were there! Born in Cleveland Ohio, from a Jewish community, but raised in California between Los Angeles and San Francisco, lived in very diverse areas of Asians, Hispanics, and Samoans, now residing in Atlanta Georgia, amongst majority of Blacks, Hispanics and Whites, I've had the opportunity to learn different people, human behavior of many different backgrounds and culture, to see we all had something in common dealing with the problem of infidelity and trust. College degree in Business and Science in 2001, but gifted and passionate to capture my thoughts and imaginations in writing into a motion picture right in the palm of your hands.

CONTENTS

Inserts from the book "Hidden Secrets of a Married man"

Charles M. Tolbert, Author

Hidden Enemy

Marriage torn by secrets of a cheating spouse. Not just cheating, but multiple secrets men keep from their wives until later revealed. Many shocking discoveries of who is the enemy, leave wives or significant others to find out otherwise what they really didn't want to know. In this story we look for answers, to see if relationships can survive the most difficult decision to trust again or take revenge that possibly can determine fate. Often people who leave from divorces are left with unanswered questions and often look for revenge, but we ask what exactly happens in this book? Was there revenge or did they forgive? Really who is this enemy? Don't assume yet, but find out the facts to the end of this story!

Who's fooling who?

This is a classic scene of a young couple, who had humble beginnings and a good start on life. Roderick, a computer programmer earns good income that gives both him and his wife Sheila a decent lifestyle. Sheila, who has a successful home business, allows her to work in her own comfort while minding the affairs of their newly purchased house in the suburbs. Roderick's terminal ill father, who's a Pastor of a prominent local church, wants Roderick his son, to soon one day take over his flock as pastor. But to the surprise of many, Roderick has a different thought in mind that would leave everyone stunned at the end. Who got fooled? Sheila? The Pastor? Roderick? Or….??

So, in this book, I prompted what is called "Pop ups!" Pop ups of the mind of suggestion and thought, that will make you wonder, but surprised at the end results. Enjoy!!

CHAPTER 1

Hidden Enemy-Trouble Knocks

AS A REGISTERED NURSE, LIVING IN A BIG CITY OF Houston Texas, it phantoms me what life may bring next. After a long 10-year marriage relationship with Michael that ended suddenly from infidelity, I didn't know which way to turn. The feeling was a moment of disbelief and a nightmare. My mind was telling me this isn't real but my eyes and ears were telling me different. I kept hearing in my mind "This is not happening" but couldn't find words to refute that thought. In a spare of a moment, I couldn't breathe from the rage that was building inside me. Once that devastation became reality, I felt my body going into shock, paralyzed from what I just seen. But let me start from the beginning of this story.

This shake up occurred one day while on a quick lunch break from work running errands to stop by the house to pick up a few things, until faced with something to my least expectation, I discovered Michael, my husband, who was supposed to be at work, in our bed with someone else. At first, upon walking in, I couldn't make out what was going on until Michael jumped up assuming that I knew… "Honey! It's not what you're thinking!" He shouted. When I actually looked at him and the bed, my mind began to race while my blood pressure rose, assuming the covered body behind our sheets and pillows be another woman. But to my discovery… "Michael Aahhhh you serious?!!" "Really?!! A man Michael?!!" The look on his face and the person he was with, was a look of a thief getting caught stealing money from his mother's purse. "But baby please it's really not what you're thinking!" (I cannot stand when someone wants to play with my intelligence or play me for a fool, plain dumb and stupid). "Thinking? Thinking Michael?!!" I shouted. "I think you two sons of a b….." "Now wait baby wait!" "Wait my a…" "Wait a minute" I said. "And you brought all this in my bed too?!!" "Oh, hell no!!" "Get out!!" "Get out before I do something terrible!!" "Do what Cheryl?" Michael asked. (Michael knows that I'm not a violent person but until today, that all changed.) "Get out before I shoot you both!" (Michael also knows that I do not lie about what I say.) "Not moving fast enough?" "I said get out of my house now before I shoot both of you.!!" "I tell you what, stay right there while I go find my gun!" (I don't even own a gun. But apparently it worked.)

I remember seeing both of them barely getting out with clothes on their back before trying to escape. After they left, I felt I wanted to throw up from looking at the bed, my sheets, pillows, and room, that once was our sanctuary now all robbed by one event I cannot swallow. Walking into our master bed bathroom, to look at myself in the mirror, trying to find out what did I do wrong, all I can see is my mascara from my eyes that once was painted pretty now running mixed between my tears. My hair that was just done yesterday, now looks like a bush from rubbing my hair constantly in disbelief. I look at my body and face and asked the very question "Was I beautiful enough for Michael not to think once he would cheat on me??" "Maybe I didn't dress sexy enough for him that made him think otherwise." "Maybe I'm too fat or too ugly or..." Then I heard myself say… "Stop it!"

I was actually blaming myself for Michael's actions. That day I felt my world ended as though someone just came and ripped it all apart from me. My family, my marriage, and my being felt worthless and all in vain. I mean I sacrificed my life for this man and worked hard to maintain this relationship to discover it was all a joke, a bad dream. What did I do to him to deserve this? For hours I walked around the whole house numb with no relief in sight, seeking but with no answers. Of course, I called the job that I couldn't return to work because of a crisis at home, then what makes matters worse, my daughter comes home from school not knowing what happened.

So, I had to play star actress, an Oscar I could had won in a spare of a moment. I could hear the school bus letting children out in the neighborhood so I looked out of the window and see my daughter coming towards the door, so I had to wipe my face from the constant tears cried earlier and pull my hair back to look like I was cleaning… "Hey baby how was school today?" "Mommy it was great!" She said. "Good baby!" "What's that in your hand honey?" I asked. She looked up at me with puppy smile eyes, happy to show me what was in her left hand while holding her empty lunch box in right, what seemed to be a posture size paper until… "Oh mommy, I painted a picture of us in our home today of you, daddy and me, you like?" Excited, she said. What more could had happened today then your own daughter to look up to a man I now hate. My thoughts and emotions were mixed if I should tell her the truth about her father, or allow her to think that he is the world and superhero of our lives.

Few hours later after Sabrina and I got settled for the evening…. "Ok honey it's time to say your prayers before going to bed." "Ok mommy" she replied. As I watched her kneel before her bed, I can see that she feels like the luckiest child in the world with her curly hair getting in the way of her eye lids touching as she tempts to pray. "God, I thank you for my teacher Ms. Smith, my friends, my fishes in my room, my daddy and mommy amen." As I watched her pray, I couldn't help but shed a tear knowing that this scene will change forever but for her sake, it lives but for tonight. Now that she's sound asleep after a few hours later, I continue to stay in her room, still in search for answers (why me?) I say to myself. I probably could have handled this better if it was one of my girl-friend's trouble. But unfortunately, it was me that got it. Finally, after walking around the whole house, only relief in sight was my daughter's room Sabrina. It gave me a sense of relief sitting in her chair beside her bed that Michael and I would normally read stories to her before she would go fast asleep.

Unfortunately, the tears return from the memories of good days, but at the same time what just took place today that would forever ruin my life. Trying to gain strength to return back to the crime scene of filth in my own bedroom, didn't have the will to do so. Instead, I sat for hours in Sabrina's room staring at the wall of a picture of me, Michael, and Sabrina wearing our favorite colors pink and black. Michael at the time looking so handsome tall cocoa butter dark skin handsome self with a nice manicured mustache in his black suit, white shirt, and pink tie that I bought for him while Sabrina and I wear our pink look alike dresses passed our knees. I can see in this picture that it was one of our happiest moments, because that day we took the picture on our 10th anniversary of marriage. But memories didn't last long that night, because of the thoughts that robbed me once again, seeking for answers and peace "what did I do to deserve this?" Needless to say, I had a breakdown that required counseling for the next two years.

The hopes of this was to help me cope with the pain and to balance my emotions from further confusion, hate, resentment, bitter, and feeling blamed for all of this. It seems now that I think about the whole matter, the only good thing I got from all of this was my daughter Sabrina now 9 years old. As time passed by and two years has gone, I did not at first had the heart to tell Sabrina what really happened between her father and I, but in time, after explaining our love has left each other without details, she understood that we had difference that caused us to go our separate ways, and she wasn't the fault for the mistakes between her father and I. Thank God, for Sabrina.

CHAPTER 2

Hidden Enemy-Moving on

NOW SINGLE PARENT AFTER 3 YEARS OF DIVORCE, I didn't know where to begin. At first, I was 18 years old when Michael and I began dating. He was the only man in my life who broke my virginity and took my heart. Wondered if anyone thought to write a manual on how to be a single parent in this age. However, one thing I did know is to get tested for any STD virus soon after the discovery of Michael's infidelity. Luckily, the results came back negative to my ease. Now 32 of age, I'm much more protective of my feelings as protective from the dating scene in fear of being hurt or come into contact with anyone with STD.

My feeling is anyone can come into contact with this disease unaware, but I do have the right to make a choice who I date. Engrossed in my job and being a single parent, has prevented me from any encounter of dating or even getting out just to have a good time singlehood. But if time did permit, don't be fooled, I'm still attractive 5'2" 130Ibs long hair red bone with hazel eyes, thanks to my Jewish heritage of my mother side, and African American by decent of my father, I'm still the most confident woman you'll ever want to encounter. So, given the chance of an encounter with someone, it won't be long until some man, or some woman's man to flirt or try to get at me.

Kim, my co-worker and girlfriend, has been trying to get me to date for months, until one day while in my cubicle at work…" "Cheryl!" "Hey Kim what's up?" "What are you doing here at work?" (Kim asked with a smirk on her face). "What do you mean by that?" "It appears to me I'm taking care of my patients who need me." I replied. "Ok, let's try this again, why are you here at work on your birthday?" Kim asked. "Well again Kim, if you must know, I'm taking care of what's important to me, that is my patients. Besides, it's just another birthday no problem, right?" I asked with puzzle look and smile. "Oh, that's where you're wrong because that's about to change." Kim said. "What do you mean by that Kim?" "I mean it's going to be different this time, because you are going out tonight to celebrate!" Kim said. "Lol, lol, lol now

Kim with whom?" I asked. "With me and the girls of course!" Kim said. "Sounds good, but I don't have a babysitter to watch Sabrina!"

Kim had that sure look as she had everything figured out. "Uhm, no need to worry, I'll have my sister watch her tonight." "Besides, she doesn't get out much but would like to spend time with Sabrina. No more excuses!" Kim said. "Ok girl, you win." I said. "But where are we going?" "It's lady's night at "Club lounge" and we are getting in free before 11pm tonight. So, dress to impress and be ready around 10pm tonight." "Oh, just one more thing… if you can't handle your liquor, let me know!" Kim said. "Girl you crazy, lol!" I said.

Later that evening, I get home from work, after picking up Sabrina from school, I hurried to my closet to pick out an outfit to wear but to no avail, can't seem to find anything that stands out. Now for you ladies that can understand, we would have a closet full of clothes and shoes, half of them still have price tag on it, yet still say "Can't find anything to wear!" Now, if you really in vanity like me, sometimes you'll forget that you would buy things for certain occasions, and if the occasion doesn't happen or went by, that outfit is done. "Forget it, I'm not going anywhere!" I said. For you men who might be reading this please understand, it's all about timing that counts, and the outfit that is appropriate for that occasion that must be right. Finally, after relentless searching, I found the right outfit perfect for the night. It was black stilettos to match with black sleeveless top and black skirt just above the knees to match. Decided to have my hair down with dark red lipstick.

Some people have told me I look like the singer Faith Evans, then others would say I look like Rihanna.

But I say I look like me…Cheryl. Finally, Kim shows up after two hours of waiting…ok getting ready to be truthful… "Girl look at you!" Kim said with excitement. You look like an expensive date no man can afford lol! "Girl shut up!" Laugh a lot I said. "Look at you with your tight blue jean pants, and all that booty hanging out, what's that old song? "Kim got a big oh butt…lol." "If you move the wrong way in them pants it might bust lolol." I said. "Ok at least I got butt lol" Kim said.

Kim's sister came inside with a warm smile… "Hey Karen!" I shouted. "Thanks for staying over to watch my baby tonight. I'm pretty sure you both will be fine." I said. "So, where's Sabrina?" Karen asked. As she toured my home, I can sense approval from her how the way I kept up the place. "Hold on Karen I will call her." I can say one thing about Karen, she is an attractive woman with dread locks tied to back of her head, with no make-up but her natural beauty makes up with anything missing along with her dimples and slight freckles on her face. I can see that she's content with who she is.

"Sabrina, come on downstairs your favorite aunt Karen is here to see you!" "Ok Mommy I'm coming!" Sabrina came running down the stairs in her newly done braided hair with the beads clacking at the thump of her feet skipping down the steps in her bright green shorts with matching color sleeveless shirt and the whitest newly purchased snickers from foot locker (boy were they expensive if I could say so myself). But she's my little princess who deserves the world. As I continued to look at her as she's coming down the stairs, I couldn't help being reminded repeatedly of her father's features, her caramel looks, her father's thick eye browse, his eyes, and nose. But with the cutest smile with lips and teeth she got from me. "Give mommy a kiss good night honey." "Ok mommy!" "Enjoy yourself Cheryl, me and the little princess will be just fine don't worry about us." Karen said. "Thank you, Karen!" "Let's go girl it's getting late!" Kim said. "I'm coming!" I said.

As Kim and I were leaving, we approached her car as it was dark could not see visibly who's in the car but certain I've noticed another person in the car..." Who is this?" I asked. "Oh, that's my cousin Angela." Kim replied. Getting into the car I greeted her cousin… But before I did, she was eager to meet me first as though I was someone special or celebrity status… "Hi my name is Angela!" "Hey, I'm Cheryl, pleased to meet you." As we greeted, I observed her looks and outfit as she is sitting in the back seat of what she is wearing, which is blue jeans, with a baby blue loud color blouse with shoes to match blouse. But for some reason to me, she didn't look the type who would put the extra effort for the night, because her hair wasn't totally attended to impress, but in a hurry of spare of a moment to get ready in last minute.

As for Kim, she's wearing a long sleeve white blouse with blue jeans that compliments her white high heels. She wears a stunning Halle Berry cut hair style, but seems to have a glow or shine like she just left the hair salon. What's different about this Halle Berry look is that she got streak of hair coming down her left eye that covers the left soul of her eye that can possibly reveal her true identity of a diva she is. But tonight, to me, she just Kim. "Girl who is your hair stylist?" I asked. "Now you know I can't tell you that, for you know we don't share that information!" Kim said. Now I know that's true, because what woman today you know would share that in fear that your hair may look better than theirs.

"Just thought I ask. Lol" I said. As we're driving off… "Kim!" I shouted. Girl I just realized that this is not the same car you had before." "When did you get this one?" I asked. Kim looked at me with a smirked as she was driving relaxed with confidence in her steering with one hand as the other on her lap. "Cheryl, where have you've been?" I traded that old Toyota car two months ago." "What is the make model of this car?" "It's the new 2008 Mercedes 300, you like it?" She asked. "Yes, girl you are doing it!" "I traded that 2004 Toyota Camry car two months ago, but same black in color." "But how can you afford it if you don't mind me asking?' I asked. "Girl I thought you knew." Kim said with confidence. "My men take good care of me." "Your men or man?" Baffled, I asked. "Oh, you heard me!" Kim said. "Men as in plural." "But why does it have to be like that?" I asked. "It's because all men are dogs and all they want is one thing out of a woman and it sure isn't to hold their hands." (I played stupid naive for a second…) "Girl you know all they want is sex, the panty, the booty, must I say more?" Kim said. "Ok, ok, I got the point Kim, lol" "yeah really so I came up with the idea and attitude all I want is the money and for someone to pay my bills for a change…!" Suddenly, the person sitting in the back seat rose from the dead, to join the conversation for reasons I don't know. Maybe it was an opportunity for someone to

HIDDEN SECRETS OF A MARRIED MAN

say the right thing that would re kindled the thought that once was incomplete now came with purpose... (I know, sounds confusing but it will come together...)

"That's right pimpin pimp them girl! Do that thing!" Angela said. I looked back in shock at Angela with surprise on my face... "Girl are you for real??" I asked. "I said right because I'm tired of these fake broke wanna be players out here and I'm about to put them all on blast!" "But don't that sound a bit scandalous?" I asked. "No girl, because they do it to us all the time with the scandalous way, they come at us." "But you said that with such animosity, lol." "Not really, because what Kim said is true, they're full of it and about tired of the..." "Whoa Angela I feel you girl." I said. "I mean just like this last boy I was with, he called himself trying to play me." "Play you Angela?" I asked. "I mean really if you going to cheat, play the game right!" "Don't leave tracks that will get you busted.

Some men are so stupid at it I think they be trying to tell you, so they can get caught." Angela said. "Let me tell you what happened, this boy Jamian my ex, he left his phone on my dresser while in my shower after having sex. A text on his phone comes through by a loud music tone and not on vibrate or silent, I was curious to see who was texting my so-called man, to find out the message was saying... "Hurry up! I'm waiting so don't forget to pick up some extra rubbers before you get here." "What?!" Kim shouted. "Girl that's crazy!" I said. "That ain't all, so I wanted to call the number to tell her a few things, but I didn't. I changed my mind by playing it off." "How did you play it off?" I asked.

"One day Jamian came by and noticed another man just leaving as he was coming in to say…" "Who was that in my woman's house and what was he here for?" "Oh him?" "Hmmm, he's my payback when you had that ho text you on your phone while you were in the shower to say don't forget the condoms!" "So, what does that got to do with this fool leaving my woman's house?" Arrogantly, Jamian asked. That fool made sure he didn't forget to bring some condoms to my house since you couldn't do that for her."

"At first, he had that look as though he wanted to hit me, but he couldn't because he knew that he was caught, out played, and didn't have much to say after that but "You got me!" lol." "So, I think Kim knows what she's talk-in about the dating life is really a pimp life." Angela said. As Kim drives, I can tell in her look after that comment Angela made about, gave her more confidence to now tell us about what pimping means… "You know Anthony and I been together off and on for the last 6 years; and during that time, we were off, I met this guy between our separation." Kim said. "We seemed at first to click well and have a lot in common until it became a business of convenience." "Business? What do you mean by business Kim?" I asked. "Well, I love Anthony, but I like my side kick too.

Gerald, pays my bills including the car note." Kim said. "But why would he really do that Kim? Isn't that like getting money for sex as a prostitute would?" I asked. I can see that Kim is getting a little irritated with my questioning but at same time shares… "I'm not a prostitute Cheryl, I'm just doing the same thing men do to us that is use us for whatever they want." "I'm playing their game, but better with perks." "A prostitute sleeps with whoever and whatever for money. I don't." Kim said.

"But what about Anthony? Does he know this?" I asked. "Girl of course not and don't need to know. It is what it is." Kim said. "That's crazy girl!" I said. "I didn't realize how far behind I was in this dating scene." As Kim is driving trying to get to the club, it got silenced for a moment until I hear noises of someone tumbling through their purse in the back… "Angela! What are you doing back there?" Kim asked. "Kim you know what time it is…I'm about to hit this and burn one real quick while sipping on this wine cooler before we get there to set the mood right. Ya'll want some?" Angela asked. "I'm good Angela." Kim said. "What about you Cheryl?" Angela asked. "Well…I'll just take the wine cooler." "Here you go girl." Angela extends a bottle of Moscato which is my favorite. "Second thought, hook me up girl!" Kim said. "But Kim, you'll be drinking, smoking and driving is that safe?" I asked. Both Angela and Kim looked at me like I just came from Mars… "Girl you should be worrying more about how you going to remember this night and hold your own liquor on your birthday lol." Kim said.

"Getting wasted! Lol" "These drinks that is waiting on you got nothing on these Moscato wine coolers." Kim said. So, we toasted to me as the birthday girl before getting to the club. As we're closely approaching the exit to turn right to the club, in eyes view I noticed plenty of cars and people all around the parking lot rushing to get in line like at an amusement park waiting to get on a spectacular advertised ride. "I don't think we're going to make it inside in time Ladies, the line is too long." Angela said with pessimism in her voice. But leave it to Kim with her tricks… "Don't worry girls I got an idea just wait here."

Kim parks the car, then rushes off to the security of guys standing, patrolling the line. Next thing I see as we're getting out of the car, Kim signals us to come to the front of the line where the security guards standing, and walked to one she knew and whispered in his ears about something as he looked at me and Angela, he nodded his head in approval, then moments later she tells us with her hand to come one, so we did, and security guard ushers us in the club. "What did you say to that guy to change his mind?" I asked. "Oh, I just told him that I knew his girlfriend, and we're close friends and how she would do something crazy if she found out that he's cheating on her at the club he works at, so just this one time let us in I won't tell and forget all about that I saw him kissing and hugging on another woman at the club last week, and it worked!"

"Now I know you crazy Kim lol!" I said. So now that we're inside the club, I can't remember seeing anything like this. I mean the last time I can remember going to something like this, when I was 21 years old, with Michael in a bar celebrating my birthday being an adult to drink for the first time. This club was quite different in view, as I browsed inside, it was full of people that look like it was over a thousand people here tonight.

The lights flashing of purple and blue, but with loud music playing and the smell of cologne and perfume combine with people talking loudly and laughing, I knew it was a place where people was either drinking their problems away or here for one-night stand. The club also had a second floor, both with bars in each corner, but one big bar in the middle. The crowd widely mixed with different races, but predominately black. The vibe of the people was full of excitement to be here, particularly the guys, because it was lady's night. The vibe did remind me again the old times when Michael and I used to get out when we were younger. "Cheryl stay here at this table, while both Angela and I get the drinks." Kim said. "But aren't you going to ask me what I want to drink?" I asked. "Oh, don't worry, I know exactly the drink to get you. Remember, it's your birthday!" Kim said. "Oh boy! That's what I'm afraid of…my birthday." I said with a sigh of confusion.

While sitting and waiting, I became self-conscious of my looks and what I'm wearing thinking I'm a bit out of date in my outfit. I thought also maybe I'm revealing too much like my skirt too tight or cleavage showing too much in fear attracting perverts or freaks. The rap music playing had a nice beat I liked for a moment "Like a lollipop!" But didn't know who's the singer, for it sure had a nice groove, until the DJ interrupts the music to say… "Tonight we got a special shot out to a beautiful lady name Cheryl, for its her birthday tonight so help me wish her a happy birthday as we play this rap song just for her…" "Go shorty, go shorty, it's your birthday, it's your birthday…we party like it's your birthday like we don't care if it's your birthday!"

The next thing I noticed comes both Kim and Angela with the bartender waiter with a big surprise… "What is all this Kim?" She decided to come back with 10 shots of vodka with assistance of Angela and a male stranger along with the waiter… "What's all this Kim?" I asked. "Cheryl, this is my friend Ronnie!" So, she introduced me to a guy I suddenly came attracted to. If I had a chance, I could have screamed just at the looks of him, 6' 3" tall tight wearing baby blue short sleeve showing off his hard work from the gym, body with arms bulging out waiting for me to touch them. His long dreads, dark clean-cut Jamaican looking guy with his pearly white teeth just my type. Ok, enough talking about him… "Hi, my name is Ronnie, but they call me Ron, happy birthday!" He said.

"Thank you and nice to meet you too!" I said with a big smile. "I heard it was your birthday, so I wanted to chip in by joining you all to a toast to the birthday Lady!" He said. So, we all were sitting at the table Kim, Angela, Ronnie, and I getting ready to toast… "I like to toast to the birthday Girl, but before I do, please allow Cheryl to bottom up!" He said. "Bottom up Cheryl bottom up!!" Excited, Angela shouted!" "What is bottom up??" I asked. The bartender who was preparing the drinks at our table began to explain how to bottom up… "Take your glass and hold it in your right hand, take the lime in your left hand and squeeze the juice between your teeth, then lick the salt around your glass, then bottom up the shot of vodka all the way, enjoy!"

I tried exactly how it was explained by the bartender. But once I drank the first glass, I felt the proof of that drink… "Are you ok??" Kim asked. "I'm ok" I said chokingly. After drinking several shots, I began to feel too happy in the moment with no cares in the world. As the night went on, several guys asked me to dance but to their disappointment, I turned them down to let both Angela and Kim dance until… "Cheryl, two guys are trying to approach our table, this time it is your turn to get up and dance!" Kim said. They treat this table like it's the hottest table asking us to dance back to back with no break." Angela said. "Don't feel like it Kim; I'm enjoying myself right here." Next thing I know, what happens, one aggressive guy that managed to squeeze through between me and Angela to ask… "You like to dance?" Kim gave me that look do it look. So hesitantly, I agreed.

After a couple of dances with same guy, my feet began to grow tired so I politely told this guy… "Thanks, I'm done!" But before I was able to turn away from him, he gently grabs my arm and hand to say… "Oh baby wait, just one more dance, then I'll let you go!" Reluctantly, I agreed. As soon as he grabs my hand for the last dance a song played by the DJ just so happened to be a slow song to my surprise, right? The song heard was T-Pain "Chopped N Screwed" "I guess this is the song we get closer, don't worry I won't bite, lol" He said. Buddy boy decides to get too close and personal by placing his arms all around my waist so tight like we're a couple or something.

Now that we're visibly eye to eye, I can now see him better close up and noticed his rough face as of a hard drinker and his eyes big and bold staring me down as if he was planning what to do next. His breath was flaming so bad even the alcohol couldn't escape. I slowly turned around so that he could be behind me, so that I could avoid being insulted from his bad breath. As we're slow dancing with a sigh of relief from his breath and look, I suddenly now can feel something hard pressing on my behind. At first, I thought it to be some object in his pants that would move soon, but it didn't go away. But it hit me suddenly to my surprise this fool got a hard on! So, I backed off slowly and turned around and said… "I'm sorry, but my feet are really killing me! Thanks for the dance." I left. But as I was leaving from him, I can see on his face of sadness and heartbroken as though he may be thinking… "Well, there goes my chance, won't be with her ever again." But had I stayed any longer, he probably would have exploded in his pants.

So, I went back to my table to meet up with the girls to find no Kim in sight but Angela. "How was it?" Angela asked. "It was ok until this pervert I was dancing with got a hard on while we were slow dancing." "What? Are you for real, lol." Angela asked. "Yes Girl, he'll never have to worry about dancing with me again!" "Oh, you still laughing Angela?" "I tell you what, let me go find him and introduce him to you, lol." "I'm good Girl but thanks, but I needed that laugh haven't laughed that hard in a while, lol" Angela said. "Anyway, where's Kim?" "Don't know probably out there dancing." "I'm going to the restroom really quick; I've been holding it too long I'll be right back Cheryl." "Ok, take your time Angela."

As I'm sitting alone at the table, I've noticed there were plenty of drinks still waiting to be had, so I helped myself to one. As time went by, I noticed again that the plenty of drinks that were once full are now empty shot glasses. I must of had at least drunk 2, 3 or maybe 4 shots, I can't remember. But what I do know is I felt tipsy, tired and feet were aching. I knew it was time for me go home, because it's late and I don't want to keep Karen babysitting

Sabrina while waiting for us to return. I hope the girls are ready to go as soon as they return back to the table.

So, I reached down the chair where I'm sitting to rub my leg and feet from aching so much, taking my shoes off, I here footsteps getting closer to my table to see an image of a person appeared before my table now in front of me. As I slowly rose up from rubbing my feet, it was a tall built dark skin man, wearing a white muscle shirt that hugged his biceps and black pants that hugged his muscle thighs like a sports athlete. At first, I thought it was Ronnie at a glance, but the more I looked, this guy was different. His face was a bold look with manicured beard that reminded me of Tyrese Gibson the actor and singer. "Hello, how are you doing?" He asked. "I'm fine and you?" I asked. "Quite well" He replied. "Are you by yourself tonight?" "No, I'm not. My Girlfriends stepped away for a moment and will be back soon." "I guess you are here to ask me for a dance, right?" "No, not really. Just thought you might need help rubbing your feet." He said. (I thought that was a cheap shot on how to pick up on someone, lol) "No, truthfully, I did want to ask if I may have this one dance with you, but first, allow me to introduce myself..." (As he was talking, I felt something different about him from all the other guys. It wasn't like any other feeling I had before). It seemed as though my heart was getting excited from the thought of looking at him and the sound of his deep charming voice that made me quiver inside...

"My name is Darryl and you?" "My name is Cheryl." "Cheryl? That's a nice name, and Cheryl where are you from?" "I'm from here a native Houston Texan, as in don't mess with Texas, lol" (ok,

I must be tipsy or drunk) "What about you? Where are you from?" I'm from Portland Oregon." "Oregon? I didn't think black people lived in Oregon lol." "Of course, they do especially in Portland." "May I sit down?" Darryl asked. (Now I really like this guy because he showed respect for me and my table unlike other guys that would help themselves) "Sure but at your own risk, lol" "I understand, lol" Darryl said. He sits right next to me while noticing all the empty shot glasses and left-over cake that was eaten earlier… "I see that you're having a goodtime tonight" "Why do you say that?" I asked being critical. "Are you assuming that these empty glasses are mine?" "Because if you are, let me tell you something, I can't stand when people… (He interrupts me to say) "Whoa hold on now!" "Don't want your blood pressure up over nothing, lol!" "It was just a joke and a kind observation."

"Now, let's try this again…I noticed empty glasses, need a drink?" (Boy, he sure knows how to make a comeback quick when it counts, he had me laughing knowing he made brownie points.) "So, what's the occasion?" "Is it divorce celebration night or just got rid of an old boyfriend that didn't appreciate a good woman?" He asked. "Those are good ones, but neither are the reasons…It's my birthday!" "Happy Birthday to the 23-year-old lady!" Darryl shouted. "Not quite, but good brownie points again. Just add 10 years to it." "What?" "No way as good as you look, I wouldn't ever guessed it!" He said with a smile. "Keep it up Darryl, you're doing good!" "Let me get you a drink so that we can toast to the birthday Girl." (I probably would had taken him up on it, but I didn't for two reasons: 1 I don't take drinks from strangers: 2 I think I had enough already…) "No thanks Darryl, it's getting late and I think I had enough drinks already." "My daughter is waiting for me to come home soon, and it's time to go." "Nice!" "You have a daughter you say?" "Yes! She is my 9-year-old princess name Sabrina." "That's a nice name, I assume this young princess is beautiful as her mother." "You know Darryl, you are saying all the right things to me, and a good salesman, because you are selling yourself well! Lol."

"Now it's my turn to ask you some questions Darryl, what brings you here tonight, alone?" "I'm kind of new here to the city and moved here a month ago to be closer to my job headquarters as a truck driver." "Now that I'm settled, I thought to reward myself by touring the city more and get out to enjoy an evening to socialize." (Just when things were perfect between Darryl and I with our conversation, placing him on cloud nine, it all went away until he told me his occupation…truck drivers have reputation of being hoes on wheels, free to sleep with anyone from city to city) "Truck driver you say Darryl?" I said in a critical judgement way.

He looked at me with surprise look in his face from my look to say… "Yes, but before you assume the worst about truck drivers, I no longer do cross country driving, but local." "Oh Darryl, I'm so sorry I didn't mean for it to come out that way…" No that's fine I can understand how you may feel about that especially being single." Darryl said. "Who said that I was single?" "Ok, sorry I just…" "I know, assumed, lol." "We must get off these assumptions tonight, lol" I said. "Ok you got me. Are you single Cheryl?" "Yes I am." But before we were able to discuss why I'm single, comes both Kim and Angela… "Hey Girl, what's going on here?" Kim asked. Darryl quickly gets up to introduce himself before I had the chance. As he extended his hand to both Kim and Angela, Kim gives me that look of approval… "Hi my name is Darryl!" "Nice to meet you Darryl my name is Kim and this is my cousin Angela."

As they continued their greetings, I happened to look at the time… It's now 1:00 in the morning. "Are you girls ready to go yet?" "To go? You are leaving now?" Darryl asked. "Before you leave, please I must have this one dance with the birthday girl!" With surprise, Kim asked… "Cheryl, you haven't danced with this gentleman yet?" "No, not yet Kim." "Well go right ahead and have this dance with Darryl, by the time you guys are finished, we will be ready to leave." Kim said with commanding voice. So, Darryl and I got up to dance together. As we began to dance the very song comes on for slow dancing… (I know, I don't want the pervert experience happening again.)

But for some reason it wasn't the case. The song played was Gerald Levert "Closure" As he held my left hand and his right hand gently touches my waist half way, our bodies did not touch but only our faces, moving to the beat which made me feel like a woman I haven't felt in a long time. But as I was dancing with him the song "Closure", I can hear the lyrics "what did I do wrong" suddenly, emotions came over me asking the very question again "what did I do wrong that caused Michael to go a different way." But before I could control myself, a burst of tears came out of know where and Darryl just looked back at me in my eyes and said it will be ok, I won't let you cry no more, I promised." After he said that,

I brought him closer to me, wrapping my arms around his neck, for security and hope this dance will never end.

At that time, I held him like a daughter would her father, then quickly felt assured this may be my future man of my life. As we're holding each other while still slow dancing, he asked me a question with a soft voice… "So, Cheryl, you never told me what you do for a living." "You didn't ask me, but since you are inquiring, I'm a RN for Houston Medical." "Ok great a nurse!" "Would this be a good opportunity for medical attention?" "I don't know, it depends if I can find you a doctor in time. Lol" After we got to know each other a little better, it's now 2:00 in the morning and the night seemed to won't end. So, I asked the big question… "So where is your wife?" "Don't have one." He said. "Ok, where's your girlfriend?" "Don't have that either." "What about your boyfriend?" (He looked at me like I must have jokes…) "I don't have that either, but if you have any suggestions in whom I need to be with let me know." He said.

"You got jokes too, lol" "Can't blame me for asking just want to make sure whom I dealing with, lol." I said. "Don't worry, because where my heart is right now is with you and nothing else matters." He said. "I like how you said that Darryl." "I don't know how or where it came from, but I felt compelled to kiss him, and the feeling from this kiss was what I expected, a connection between us. It flowed, with energy and comfort I long waited for. "What just happen Darryl?" "I don't know Cheryl, it just felt right I guess." "I'm sorry Darryl, I didn't mean for that to happen." "It's time that we leave, I know that they are waiting" I said. "Right, let's go before they get impatient looking for you." "Wait! Before we go back, here's my number call me." I said. "I was going to ask for that before you leave, but you beat me to it. I will call you tomorrow." Darryl said.

Now that we made it back to the table, I can see it was clear that they were ready to go with purses in hand… "I see you two have gotten well acquainted with each other." Kim said. "Yes, we did." I said with a smile. Finally, we all managed to leave the club along with Darryl our escort to the car, he shook my hand as well as he did with both Kim and Angela. I didn't disclose what happened between Darryl and I, our kiss and exchanging numbers, but I can see that look on their face anticipating me to kiss him as we were leaving but to their disappointment, just a handshake. While leaving the club, I can see Darryl standing there making sure we drive off safely. As Kim is driving, she looked at me all pumped up with a thousand questions I knew was coming… "Ok Girl, spill it!" I had an innocent look on my face as I sat next to her in front passenger seat looking straight ahead… I can sense her mind is racing wanting to know with curiosity what happened.

"Spill what Kim?" Kim with a straight look on her face as she is driving, her mind continues to run with curiosity… "You know what I'm talking about so don't play stupid and innocent now!" "Your new venture we just left back there at the club." "Oh, you mean Darryl?" "Hmm, nothing really-I mean we had a couple of dances and that was it." "No Girl! That ain't true!" Kim said. "Come on now tell us what really happened." Angela asked. "I sensed chemistry between the two of you." Kim said. "Alright you two!" "So, we did have a little chemistry! That only happened because I liked the conversation that ended up with me giving my telephone number…" "Did he ask for it?" Angela asked. "No!" "I just felt it was the right thing to do."

"I can't believe you actually did that!" "I can't believe how he got through to you Cheryl? I mean you was cold to many of the guys both from work and anywhere else we went but this guy?" Kim asked. "I need to talk with him and ask how did he break the ice woman, lol." Kim said. "So, what does he do for work?" Angela asked. "He's a truck driver." It got silent for a moment until… "A truck driver." I said under my breath. "He's what?" Kim asked. "A truck driver Angela, truck driver!" "Ok, I had some reservations about this too about his occupation." "Girl, I know that you know that truck drivers sleep with everything and anything in every city they go, but get that out of your head because not all of them do that." Kim said. I was certainly surprised to hear that coming from her and didn't expected.

"Follow and listen to your heart say, and get to know him more before you decide to rule him out." (That's why I like Kim, because although she talks crazy and do things I wouldn't do, but she can say something with much wisdom that even a counselor would want to hire her.

Now pulling up to my place to park, I can see Angela passed out from the ride and drinks, Kim turns off the car engine than looks over at me with a serious look on her face like a mother would at her daughter… "Listen, I know it's been hard on you after your last breakup with Michael, and how he broke your heart and left you scars for life. But you can't continue to look for excuses

Cheryl." "What do you mean by that Kim?" "I mean not giving yourself a chance at love again." "I know Kim, but he really hurt me and messed up my life to ever wanting to trust another man. I'm suspicious of men who ever may try to come into my life, in fear I would run into something like this again." "I understand Cheryl how you feel, but everyone is not Michael and would do the same thing to hurt you again." "Remember, keep your mind clear and your heart open, for you never know what good you may invite in." Kim said. Once I heard that from Kim, I paused with a sigh and agreed… "Thanks Girl, I needed that!" "I'll sleep on it and give it more thought later, but for now the night is done and in the books. I'll talk to ya'll later" We hugged and kissed each other on the cheek… "Love you Cheryl!" "Love you too Kim and say bye to Angela for me while I go get Karen to come out so she can finally go home." "Ok tell her I'm waiting outside." "Later Girl!" I said.

CHAPTER 3

Who's Fooling Who? –
The Emergency Call

"WHAT ARE YOU WATCHING?" SHEILA ASKED. "Watching the basketball playoffs." Roderick said. "Oh yeah! Who's playing?" "The Los Angeles Lakers against Detroit Pistons, Lakers up by 4 points in the 3rd quarter with little under two minutes, and Kobe Bryant holding the ball…yes, I'm going for the Lakers, any more questions?" Roderick said with sarcasm. "Ok, Mr. smart mouth, see if you will be sleeping on the couch tonight!" Sheila gently pushed Roderick's forehead back as she was leaving the couch, from sitting next to him before passing him by… "Silly!" Sheila said. "Why you hit me on my head Sheila? Can't you see

I'm trying to watch a peaceful game and you want to get violent!" Roderick said. "Boy stop complaining I just pushed your head with my fingers, you know that." Sheila said with a smirk. "See Sheila that's your problem you play too much." "Whatever Rod, lol." "Anyway, I'm getting something to eat, did you want anything while I'm in the kitchen?" "Yeah, since you are in the playing mood, pass me them bag of Doritos on top of the fridge, and a cold beer." Sheila reaches for the chips as she looked at him with another smirk while reaching for the beer in the refrigerator. "Here you go!" "Thanks baby!" "I thought you said you were going to cut down on drinking?"

"Remember what happened to your uncle Drew, and how he couldn't handle his liquor getting drunk, pulling people over by honking his horn in his beat-up truck, like he was still the police after retirement 20 years ago, lol." "Yeah that was crazy, but I can handle mines." Roderick said with confidence. "Well keep drinking them beers, sooner or later, you will have that big belly like your Uncle, lol" "You got jokes but for now, enjoy this six-pack stomach while you can, lol" "So, don't hate, besides I didn't hear you complaining the other night when we got it on, after drinking a beer." Roderick said. "Oh, don't even flatter yourself, in that case, you'll need a 40' ounce or two…" Sheila said. "Ok, ok, keep talk'n!" "We'll see about that Sheila!" "Yeah, we'll see alright superman Rod!"

"Hey, since we are talking while your game is on commercial, don't forget about next week." "Next week?" "What's next week?" "Quit playing I'm serious Rod, you know what's next week, I mean what are we going to do?" "I don't know what we're going to do, but I know what I'm going to do (Roderick nods his head in confidence). "Oh really? Like what?" "I'm planning to take out this fine lady I've been knowing for some time." "Oh yeah? Please tell me who this person is." (Sheila's curiosity rises for answers…) "Yeah, we're gonna kick it at this spot I picked out I know for sure; she will like it." "And where's this at so I can tell you if really she will like it." "Oh, I can't tell you that because it's a secret and I know how you women like to gossip and talk assume whatever." (Sheila smacked her teeth and rolled her eyes at Rod) "Look, just tell me and I'll tell you for sure if she will like it or not." "Nice try baby but no, and that's my final answer as the game plays…" "I think I got this one, and besides it might just get back to my wife, about it being our 6th year wedding anniversary."

"Boy you are so silly! Lol" "I need to kick your butt for that one, come here…!" "No, you come here Sheila!" (She walked toward him while he was sitting on couch and jumped on him to horseplay wrestle on the couch…) "Sheila what are you doing? Can't you see I'm still trying to watch the game! Lol." "I'm going to get you Rod for that!" "Oh no baby, you too short to reach me. Lol" "I'll reach you alright!" (Roderick got up to try to run away from her, while being chased around the coffee table in the living room…) "Stop playing Sheila for real, lol!" Finally, Roderick gave up by falling back on the couch to let Sheila have dominancy over him… "Girl what are you doing?"

"What it looks like…?" Sheila grabs Roderick's arm in attempt to hold him down, but Roderick's strength only frustrated her more, but continued to try to hold him down. "I told you what I'm going to do!" (She grabbed his ears and squeezed it while Roderick grabbed her by the waist with force close to him as she was on his lap…) "You can't win Sheila, so you might as well quit trying while you are still ahead! Lol" "You're right Roderick, since you are nothing but big log on my couch! (Panting)."

"Your couch? Last I checked I'm the one who paid for it." Roderick said. "Oh, so why we got to go there, gotta be like that? Ok, last I checked I'm paying the rent! Now what you got to say! Lol." Sheila said. "Whatever Sheila!" "Oh, you want some more butt whooping? Come here!" "Stop Sheila my game still on, lol!" "I'm not through with you yet!" (They continued to tussle on the couch until the phone rang…) "The phone is ringing Sheila!" "Ok, go answer it! Sheila said (panting). "You get it Sheila; besides it could be your boyfriend calling, lol!" "Boy stop!" (Sheila gets up to run to the kitchen to answer the phone…)

"Hello…" Roderick is slowly getting back into the game now it's 4th quarter and Laker's up by 2 before it's final, until …) "Yes, this is the Jackson's residence who's calling?" (A long pause came from Sheila that changed once a happy childhood looking face to now confused with great concerns…) "He's what?" (Roderick's focus on the game in last minutes sensed something was wrong more important to look toward Sheila's face as he contemplated what was more important…) "What's going on Sheila?" (Sheila doesn't answer)

"When did this happen?" "What Sheila what?" The game has shifted from Roderick's focus to now in hasty anticipation of the phone conversation… "We're on our way – thank you!" Sheila hangs up the phone and looks at Roderick with troubled but sympathy look… "What Sheila What? Just tell me!" "Your Father had a stroke, and now is in the emergency room being operated on." (The look on Roderick's face was of shock and traumatized as though someone tried to kill him…) "Roderick snap out of it; we must go now!!"

CHAPTER 4

Hidden Enemy –Phone Encounter

IT'S NOW BEEN SIX DAYS SINCE I LAST MET DARRYL AND spoke with him, not knowing if I will ever hear from him again, or find out if he's still interested in me. It was one evening Sabrina and I just made it home after a long day at work and coming from a PTA group meeting at Sabrina's school… "Mommy, your phone is ringing!" Sabrina hears my phone, because I normally would leave my keys and phone on kitchen counter where she would begin to do her homework, but what amazes me is that I just put that phone down not knowing if anyone would call me at that time of the evening after 7pm.

"Mommy your phone is still ringing!" Sabrina shouted. "Don't worry honey, let it go into voice message I'll get it later, I'm busy right now!" I shouted across the hall from my bedroom to the kitchen… "Trying to take quick shower honey I'll get it later…!" "Ok Mommy!"

After getting settled for the evening an hour later, after a shower and meal, I finally had the chance to hear my voice messages on my phone while relaxing on the couch watching TV; I noticed two missed calls that came from a number that I didn't recognize, until I played the message back, the voice sounded familiar but couldn't put the name to it until I hear… "Cheryl!" "This is Darryl, we've met in a club about a week ago, and wanted to call to see how you were doing, and to wish you a good evening and to feel free to…"

Before I was able to hear the rest of the message, I hurried to call him back by dialing his number… "Hello!" "Hi Darryl it's me Cheryl, how are you doing?" (My heart was beating so fast with excitement I had to catch my composure not letting him know I was excited to hear from him.) "Great Cheryl now that I hear your voice."

As he was talking, I noticed more his voice, how sexy it was, that sent me chills up my back, I didn't want to hang up the phone anytime soon. "So How do you like the night life of Houston?" I asked. "Well, it's quite different from Portland as far as the weather is concerned, but for the people, they are no different from where I came from." (As he's talking, my mind goes back to remind me that he's a truck driver and he gets around especially with the women…) "So, what do you mean by that Darryl?" I asked. "White folks will be white and black folks will be black. Jobs, white folks get the good paying jobs, while blacks get less, crime justice is in more favor of white crime than black crime getting leniency, and because of better pay, whites have better chance of home ownership than blacks. It seems to be the epidemic no matter where you live or what state you reside."

"Wow Darryl do you really feel that way?" "Don't you think it's a little unfair to stereotype? Remember, no matter what color or race you are, we all have choices in life, and for every choice there's consequences whether it be good or bad." I said. "Maybe you are right Cheryl. I can be little bias in my thinking, but at the same time I've gotten around different cities to see the things similar that I've seen elsewhere." Darryl said. "So, what do you think of Houston now that you've been here a minute?" "I don't know yet, and I don't want to say something or assume something without further getting more experience of the city before truly speaking how I feel. But so far, it has been positive experience."

"Well for the most part, we are positive people who try to be kind to our neighbors." "As a matter of fact, this is the city where Beyoncé was born and raised, the Bush city of former Presidents with that name, and oil we claim." "This city has given me as a single parent, divorced Jewish/Black woman, an opportunity to make a change by completing medical school and to get a well-paying job as a nurse." "Although this city has its fair share of crime like anywhere else, it affects all walks of life as well as the blacks, Jews and of all races."

"So, you are Jewish mixed? I didn't know that!" Darryl asked. "Yes, I am." "My mother is full Jewish and my father is black!" "He met her during the Vietnam War as she attended the wounded soldiers as a nurse during that time; fortunately for him, he was wounded and met the love of his life that turned out to be 46 years of marriage to his death, 5 years later after his death, my mother passed away." "What I've learned from my parents is courage and fight, my mother had much courage to do what she did, and my father had much fight to protect what was right to him."

"So, I've been taught to embrace all races." "Besides, we have a lot of educated black owners and prominent black owned business all around. So, you can't pass judgement on your experiences alone." "Ok, ok, I think I got your point!" Darryl said. "Remind me the next time I decide to get into the political or controversial subject, to vote for you, lol." Darryl said. "Funny Darryl! I see you got jokes…lol"

"Anyway, let's get down to business why we are even talking." Seriously I said. "You are an attractive man and I think you know that, so tell me about your past relationships before I want to have you as a friend." "Oh, ok a friend I see, that's what's up Cheryl." "Ok answer my questions before you decide to use sweet words to try winning me over." Seriously I said. "Are you married? Divorced? Or what? I mean I know I ask you once before, but I really want to know the truth."

"Wow!" "21 questions…lol" Darryl said. "Yeah, and it's about to be 22 if you don't answer, lol" Cheryl said seductively but serious. "Ok, since you put it that way, (Darryl clears his throat) well, my last serious relationship I had was back in Portland, it lasted for 6 years, and she was my fiancé until… (Darryl paused) "Until what Darryl?" "She was killed by a stray bullet that punctured right into the side of her stomach and back that killed also my unborn child." "She was pregnant Darryl? "Yes, she was." "I haven't gotten completely over it, until last year when I decided to move away from the state and city, in order to have a fresh start from the past."

"I'm so sorry Darryl!" "I didn't know, and to come on strong with questions…" "It's ok, like I said, I've managed to heal from it and move on." "I'm good, at least I can talk about it." "If you don't mind me asking one more question Darryl?" "Go ahead and ask." "How did you find out and how did this stray bullet come about?" "Well, I was working on my car underneath my truck changing the oil, until I heard noises and screeching of tires, so I stopped what I was doing to roll out from beneath my truck to investigate the noise I just heard which was not normal, to find and discovered my fiancé soon to be wife, covered in blood looking at me with her last breath trying to tell me something that I couldn't figure out at that time until later after she passed, my mind and heart was saying I love you." "It tore me to pieces and didn't know how to react at the moment…"

"Are you ok Darryl? I can't hear you." "It's ok, ok to cry I'm here for you." "Why did she have to leave so soon!" "She was my heart and was pregnant with my first son, I didn't have the chance to kiss or hold him. (crying)" "I'm so sorry, Darryl, you sound like you would had been a good father to him." "This is such a sad story…" "It is, but now I know all she ever wanted was for me to be happy…" Cheryl took a deep breath with thoughts of empathy… "Anyway, after the funeral, I lived with regrets and guilt from not being there to protect her. I haven't dated any other woman since her."

"What was her name Darryl?" "Laura Stevenson, because my last name is Stevenson. She was my true love. Since then, I stayed single until I knew I was over the hurt of her being gone." "That's an amazing story to hear Darryl – I mean, I thought I was the one with problems or problem relationships with fear about getting into another one." "To be honest Darryl, I haven't been with any other man since my divorce over 3 years ago, or even talk to another man until…" Cheryl pauses… "Until what Cheryl?" "Until now, I don't know what it is about you Darryl, but it all seems different from my past relationship."

"I must say the same about you Cheryl; I mean since I saw you in the club, I couldn't take my eyes off of you, not that you reminded me of any other woman or even my past fiancée, but it was a vibe or energy that drew me to you out of everything else." "Oh, really?" "Yes, Cheryl really, I mean it's like fate has brought us to this point like it was meant to happen." "I feel it is more than a physical attraction." "Explain yourself Darryl when you say physical attraction, I mean what was it physically that you liked?" (I want to hear this one.) "Well, it's obvious you have physical attraction that any man would want. You have a body that draws any blind man to see, then also you have swag, a sexy swag for a conservative type of woman." "I mean, your long hair and looks was different from the average black woman, now I know that you are Jewish and black, it did stand out different from others!" "Don't get me wrong, I adore and embrace the women of my culture, but I guess in your case, I was intrigued of your difference of beautiful flowers or fruits, that one man can capture." Darryl said.

Cheryl frowns from the comment made by Darryl to say… "Why is it that black women got to have long hair?" "I think it's an insult to black women all together!" "You probably wouldn't had noticed me if I had short hair and kept on walking, wouldn't you??" I said. "Lol, lol, lol!!" "What's so funny Darryl?" "I'm not laughing." "I'm serious Darryl!" "What's funny is you got a lot of fight that came from your father in you, that needs to come out." "So, whenever you have time, you are welcome to come to my house and we can get some boxing gloves and box it out in my backyard, lol."

"Real funny Darryl." "It may be funny to you, but I was being serious." "But Cheryl, what you fail to understand is I like that in a woman." "I admire a woman who stands up for what she believes in." "Besides, it wasn't just the hair I noticed…" Darryl paused. "What else Darryl?" "Baby got backs! Lol." "Lol, lol, now I know Darryl that you are crazy and stupid, lol! "You sound just like any man no matter what race, ya'll just like the booty, lol!" "Ok, ok you got me, I may have been attracted to all that butt…I mean…, but, besides…" "Darryl it sounds like you are stumbling over your words, are you ok? Do you need a speech therapist?"

"Funny Cheryl, but really what I mean is I like the conversations we had that night and the one we're having right now." "Oh really?" "Why do you say that Darryl?" "Because you make me feel that I can be myself and not hide or cover up." "We've been on the phone for the last three hours enjoying each other, and now that I think about it, I must excuse myself for a moment for I must take care of some business." "Some business Darryl? Oh, like your girlfriend is calling and waiting on you?" "No Cheryl, if you must know, I must go to the restroom and take a leak." "Oh, how nice that the little boy must go and twinkle, lol!" "Real funny Cheryl, real funny." "Ok, take me with you." Darryl's look on his face with shock… "Are you serious?" "No Cheryl that's not a gentlemen thing to do just hold on I'll be right back…!" Darryl returns from the restroom to pick up the phone… "Hello, hello, hello, are you still there Cheryl?" Darryl hears a settled sound in background noise of a toilet flushing… "Hello Darryl, you there?" "I'm here baby, lol" "What's so funny?" "We both had to go but you didn't want to tell me trying to be all lady like, lol" "Ok Darryl you got me, lol" "You see, I like that Cheryl, we can be ourselves instead of hiding." "I understand what you are saying Darryl, but you also must remember that this is our first phone conversation and I am a lady so I don't want you to think I'm not, or up on my cleanliness as a lady that I am." "I already know that you are a Lady." "I heard in the background water you washing your hands." "What? You did?" "Yes." "I know you are really crazy Darryl, lol!"

"It makes me think how it could be in the bedroom…" "Bedroom Darryl??" "What does washing your hands got to do with bedroom??" "Umm, nothing I was just thinking of something else that suddenly became irrelevant that didn't tie into this conversation, but anyway, what about us going out on a date for dinner or something, wouldn't that be nice?" "That would be nice Darryl!" "What do you have in mind?" "I don't know Cheryl, since I'm still new in town maybe you would have suggestions." "I do, you like steak?" "Yes, I do." "There's a steakhouse restaurant so happened to be called "Houstons" "I love their steaks and how tendered it is." "They are good and the service is wonderful, but it could be a little expensive, so maybe we can try…" Darryl interrupts to say… "We will do Houstons!" Cheryl paused… "Ok, when?" "Let's try this Friday night at 8:00pm." "Ok Darryl that's sounds good, I'll be ready." "Oh, by the way, dress to impress, because I certainly will." "Oh, don't worry, I got this!" "You sure do with that long hair and that…" "Bye Darryl!" (Cheryl interrupts) "Bye Darryl! Lol"

"Bye you say??" "No, but a goodnight." "Ok, goodnight Darryl and sweet dreams!" "Ooh you said that so sweet Cheryl, say it again, lol" "Ok, good night Darryl, may your dreams come true!" Cheryl said seductively in her voice. "Ooh, I like that good night, rest for sure, it will be a happy night, lol" Darryl said. "Ok Cheryl, have a good night too, see you soon…"

Months later after frequent dates and talking over the phone, didn't take long to become intimate, lovers, and deep friends that resulted a strong bond in the relationship. Both Darryl and I at times became inseparable where we would find ourselves almost doing everything together that included shopping and going to the grocery store together, from dentist appointments to even getting the car serviced.

We were indeed inseparable unless times his jobs would require him travel out of the state for a short mandatory assignment, to be away for weeks at a time. It didn't take long for my guard to come down from past speculations of what truck drivers may do on idle time, but what overshadowed that thought was how he showed love for my daughter Sabrina, and how he took time out to spend with Sabrina.

Although it may sound like a fairytale, it doesn't always pan out to be, for it doesn't take long for the devil to show his ugly head… It was one Sunday afternoon, Sabrina and I just made it back from church, there was a message that said… "Cheryl, this is Michael! How's Sabrina my baby daughter? I have something to tell you, so you need to get back with me at this number as soon as possible."

After hearing that message, it startled me for a moment in being reminded of the horrific event I saw that caused the relentless scars I still hold. I sat down after feeling dazed like someone just suckered punched me. Reluctantly, being reminded of the anger and bitterness I still hold against Michael, scratching my head asking myself "Why now, why!"

The anger increased after intense thoughts and frustration from being interrupted and ripped from the bliss of happiness I was enjoying until the thief came to steal it without invitation. With anger, I threw the phone down with such force, that the impact cracked the screen cover of my phone… "Great!!, now I need a new phone!" "How dare he call me now after 3 years of silence and neglect of his financial obligations to his own daughter!" "After all I went through and the scars, he put me through was once healing until now reopened. Thanks Michael, you devil!! For taking away any forgetting you was ever in my life!" "You think I'm going to call you back now? I don't think so…"

CHAPTER 5

Who's Fooling Who?
Tragic Memories

AFTER THE FRANTIC CALL, BOTH SHEILA AND Roderick hurried to get ready, to go to the emergency room at nearby hospital where Roderick's father was, as they proceeded to the car "Give me the keys Rod!" Roderick couldn't drive so Sheila took over the wheel, because of the nature of the shock, Roderick's focus wasn't there for fear of the worse... "Are you ok Rod?" Sheila asked while slowly caressing Roderick's hand, as she drove and steered the wheel with her left hand. "I'm ok." Roderick said softly with emotions of memories flowing through his mind remembering what happened to him as a child... "It feels like Deja vu all over again" He said.

Roderick thinks back in his mind, as he sits in a daze to remember… (It was 1996, the song Tupac playing "Ain't mad at ya" I was 12 years old singing repeatedly to myself in the mirror while looking at my chest… "I think my muscles getting bigger!" I would pose like I'm the Incredible Hulk or something. "I must be getting taller or grown another inch, let me go see." I would get my marker to check off the last mark to see… "Nope, I guess not." "I think one day I will be taller than my father and become a famous basketball player with my favorite team the Los Angeles Lakers."

As I continued my vanity venture, a sudden shout came from downstairs… "Roderick hurry up!!" "We're going to be late!!" "You know your father is expecting you to be on time for your water baptism, so hurry up!!" "Ok, ok Mama I'm coming!" "Man, what is the big deal about all of this?" All I'm doing is getting wet in some cold water for a minute, and for me to have to change clothes all over again. I don't know why he's doing this, but maybe so he can show off in front of his church as the new pastor.

He ain't fooling nobody. He keeps telling me I'm going to take over his church one day and be the next pastor, but that is something he wants, not me… "Hurry up Roderick!!" "We're already late!! "I said I'm coming Mama!" (She's starting to get on my last nerve with this, ain't like I wanna go anyway.)

I stumped slowly down the stairs while Mama is staring at me by the door… "Boy, what has gotten into lately?" "Get in the car now!" As we're driving off and Mama speeding, she glimpses over at me to say… "Talk to me, what's wrong with you lately?" "Nothing Mama!" As I sat looking down between my legs moping to say… "Mama why are we doing this?" "Doing what son?" "I mean this trying to please Dad, knowing I don't care about what he wants." "I mean he reminds me all the time that one day I'm going to do this job when I really want to do something else when I grow up."

I remember the look on my mother's face as she hurried through traffic, it was of focus but sensitive to my feelings the same time to ask… "What is it that you want to do baby when you grow up?" "I'm going to be a famous basketball player." I can remember her look on her face raising her eyebrows with surprise… "Oh really?" "And what team would you play for if you don't mind me asking?" "Come on Mama really?" "The Lakers Mama the Lakers, you see my room with Laker postures everywhere, come on Mama, lol"

I can remember my Mama laughing to ask… "But whatever happened to Chicago Bulls? You know Michael Jordan needs some help; don't you think?" "No Mama, I think the Lakers needs me more after Magic Johnson left." As we were talking, I continued to notice Mama speeding more… "Mama don't you think we need to slow down? I think you are speeding too much." "Son, I got this relax; so, tell me more why did you choose the Lakers over your home team Chicago where you were born and raised on the southside?" "Because I feel I have a better chance to be popular as a star in California than here. I would have more girlfriends out there who would like me."

"You so silly my son, lol" "Girls are going to like you for you, not for who you play for." While Mama drives, I look out the window gazing watching how many cars we could pass up and the neighborhood trying to count the number of girls that are pretty from the one's that wasn't until Mama broke my concentration to say… "Now listen quickly, when we get to the church, I want you too… "Ma, lookout for that bus!!!" I shouted. AHHHH! MAMA!!!!" "Lord help me now, AHHH" My mother screamed. From once a speeding smooth ride has now ended by the sudden impact that collided with a bus, I blacked out and couldn't remember a thing.

Later… "Where am I?" "My eyes… I can't see!" All I can remember is that I felt numb and I'm sitting somewhere in a cold room not knowing what's around me until I hear a voice… "Young man just take it easy." "It's going to be ok." "As you know, you're one of the lucky ones that survived that accident." "What accident?" "You don't remember?" "Of course not, because it was a sudden tragic and too much trauma on your body to remember. After all, the bus took the car and tore it into shreds." "It was said that it was luck there were any survivors from that car, but by the time you made it to the hospital there were vital signs of recovery in progress, it was a miracle that you made it through." "What's wrong with my eyes I can't see anything." "Can you see me in front of you son?" "I see light and feel you near me but I can't really see." "If you can see me, then it's because your eyes are a little fuzzy right now from the glass that shattered all over your face." "My face?" "Mama what happened and where's Dad?"

I can remember a pause from not hearing her talk but a hear of a sigh… "Son, your father is right outside the door on his way in to see you." "But Mama where are you going?" All I can remember is a kiss on my forehead and a whisper to my ear… "It's going to be ok" She rubbed my head and slowly walked away until I can hear my father say "Thank you Ma'am I will take it from here." The door closes. "Dad?" "Yes, son it's me." "I can hear him sitting next to me and holds my hand very tightly. "Son how do you feel?" "I feel ok Dad, but I can't see too well, and I can't feel my legs." "Well son, in a few days it will get better." "You've suffered two broken legs deep cuts to your face from shattered glass, and head trauma that left you in a short coma the last two weeks." "It was said that you weren't going to make it, but I prayed to God that you would, and you did, thank God."

I can remember Dad continued to talk until I interrupted him to ask him… "Dad, dad! Where's Mama and why she leaves the room?" I can sense that Dad must had lean back into his chair with great sigh of grief… "Son, your mother passed away from the accident and we had her funeral last week!" I can remember the feeling of hurt and anger that overwhelmed my injuries, after hearing this news. I couldn't really move because my body felt numb. But if I was able to move, I would had jumped up and screamed, maybe hit the wall or something but I just couldn't. I tried shedding a tear but from the heavy bandages all over my face and body, I felt like a living mummy.

I can feel my body shake because it wanted to move from the news but couldn't. "Now son take it easy you are only hurting your body." "But why, why this is happening? What did I do to deserve this?" "Now son calm down, your mother is in a better place and we should be thanking God that she is now in Heaven." "We cannot blame God for every casualty that happens." "For it is God's will that we be safe and live, not die."

"Unfortunately, your mother made poor choices by speeding and not listening to her conscious to slow down while driving, before getting a ticket or even worse an accident." As Dad was speaking, I could vaguely remember Mama was speeding, she was digging into her purse at the same time to tell me something, until it all blacked out. I remember looking up in the ceiling of the hospital to say to myself "Why God, why?" "This wasn't supposed to happened!" "I wouldn't had lost my Mama if I just hurried up like she said. It's my fault. No, maybe my Mama would be living now if it wasn't for Dad's wish for me to be baptized. For a moment, I looked at dad with sudden hate in my eyes, to say "It's Dad's fault my mama not here!"

CHAPTER 6

Hidden Enemy – Kim's Story Pimpess

THE NEXT DAY WHILE AT WORK, I RAN INTO KIM TO tell her what happened… "Kim, guess what?" "Guess who called me last week!" Kim steady typing on her computer while in her cubicle to say… "Girl stop bragging about Darryl again, don't you think I know that you two like each other by now?" "No Kim, it's not that." "I get a message from someone of the past that I haven't heard from in a while." Kim's focus stops from hitting another key on her keyboard to look up at me to ask... "Voice Cheryl? What voice from the past, like who?" "It was Michael."

"Michael?" Suddenly the face that was focused earlier on paperwork changed into a face of judgement ready to smash and trash talk... "Oh that dead beat who don't know to be a man or woman Michael?" "Yes, Girl, lol!" "What does he all of a sudden want?" "Come back home to be a man? It's too late for that." "He should had told you that he wanted to be a with another man instead of leading you on these many of years." "Where's the respect in that Cheryl?" "That's what pisses me off about some of these men." "I got more respect for someone who wants that life than to cover it up and pretend that they are someone else, especially in a marriage, right?" Kim said.

"Yes, Girl you are right." "Ok, what did he really want?" "I don't know, but it's probably something to do with Sabrina, his child." "He left a message saying to call him immediately." "Hmm, I don't know what to say about that one Cheryl, maybe child support caught up with him, who knows." "You think Kim?" "I don't know, but if he's calling now, it better be something to do with money." "You are right Kim; I hope so too." "Because it seems like every time, I try to get child support from him, he would quit his job in time to avoid garnishment from his check, then disappear for a while." "At some point, I just got tired chasing him down and try making it on my own."

"But why Kim, does it got to be like that with some of these men? Why do they always put the kids in the middle of their mess, by not doing their job as a parent supporting their children?" "It's not just that Cheryl, they do not know how to be a pimp without tracks and still able to take care their family." "Comm 'on Kim, let's be more serious about this." "No, no, Cheryl I am serious." "You got to let them know that you ain't for free and Darryl needs to know that too… (Kim looked at me with curiosity in her eyes) "Did you give up the booty to Darryl? And if so, how soon did you give it to him? Was it good? Was it quick like some instant toast pop up less than five minutes?" "Stop it Girl, you making me laugh too hard, lol" "I'm for real Cheryl, if you really did give it up, then he needs to be paying some of your bills." "I mean, how many times I have to tell you Cheryl to stay ahead of the game."

"Ok, ok, ok Kim." "Since you got it like that and all the answers, when did you decide to give up the booty to Anthony or the married guy Gerald?" "Oh, Girl let me tell you how that came about. I mean really, I liked Anthony, and it didn't take maybe two months or so, but with Gerald, I think it was two weeks…" Kim said.

"Two weeks?" "Two weeks Kim like really?" "Yes, two weeks! Don't act like you're so surprise at that." Kim defended. "Now you know there are people out there giving it up less than a week if not one day." Kim justified. "But what was so special about Gerald that made you give it up sooner than with Anthony?" "Oh, it was how he came directly with what he wanted with no sugar coating or beating around the point." "He presented himself at the right time when Anthony and I was separated broke up for the moment. If it had been any other time, this wouldn't have worked."

"So, don't be thinking I'm promiscuous or something because I don't be doing that kind of stuff giving it up to just anyone Cheryl." Kim said. "One day this guy approached me at the grocery store and said something to my least expectation." "What did he say Kim?" I asked inquisitively. "He said something like… "Pardon me Ms. Lady, I don't mean to interrupt your shopping, but I couldn't let this opportunity pass me by without at least asking if I can simply be adult enough, mature enough without insulting your beauty and intelligence, by asking for one evening sharing ecstasy with you in a place that will steal all of our troubles away for a short period that would give an everlasting memory of pleasure."

"What, for real Kim! Lol" "Yes, I mean after he said all that, I looked at him intently to see how well he was dressed, average looking guy, but knew how to look like a million dollars in his blue two piece suit like he just came out of a meeting, expensive looking glasses that complimented his gentleman look and well-manicured mustache and curly short well cut hair, I was impressed." "So, when I heard all of that, and how his voice sounded very sweet but professional at the same time, I almost felt compelled to give him the panties right there and then…" "Girl stop it! Really Kim like really? Lol" "I mean who could say no after all that Cheryl?" "I betcha you would had done the same thing too, Right Cheryl?"

"Umm, no Kim, lol!" "Whatever Cheryl, anyway, so guess what he does next after that, he offered to buy all my groceries that day so I took advantage of it, selecting mostly name brand, instead of generic brand, the expensive meats and you know I had to at least get three bottles of my favorite wines. I think that bill came up to

$600.00 dollars!" "Now I know that you are really crazy Kim, lol!" "I couldn't help it, his talk and charm were the right moment, that made him win the lottery with me, so I fell for it, we went out, and we had a good time like he said. In fact, I gained more from him, because he always gives me money and I don't even ask for it." "So, Kim if he's doing all of this, for what in exchange?" "Oh, you know Cheryl we talked about it before in my car going to the club remember?" "Oh yes, right." "So, Cheryl, if things don't work out between you and Darryl let me know, maybe I can get one of Gerald's rich friends to hook up with you!" "Ok Kim, I'm through…Bye Girl! lol" I finally walked away from Kim's pimp story, which I think is crazy especially if the man is married. Well, more power to her…back to work!

CHAPTER 7

Who's Fooling who – At the Hospital

BOTH SHEILA AND RODERICK ARE NOW AT THE HOSPI-tal, as they hurried to the front desk of the emergency room… "May I help you?" Front attended asked. "We're here to see Mr. Palmer Jackson." Roderick panted. "What's your relationship with him Sir?" "I'm his son Roderick Jackson, and this is my wife Sheila." "Please have a seat, someone will be with you in a moment." "A moment? He may not have a moment; I need to see him now!" Roderick shouted frantically.

"Look Sir, I understand how you feel but the Doctor is currently with your father and he's been notified of your arrival and will be with you momentarily." "Look, all I need to know if my father is ok?" "Sir all I can tell you is that he's currently in surgery and no one is allowed in the operating room until the Doctor gives permission." Sheila tries to calm him down by embracing and rubbing her 6'4" tall masculine husband, with her hand to his chest against her 5'6" petite feminine body as they sobbed, not knowing what to expect. "Come on honey, let's go have a seat until the Doctor arrives." Sheila said softly. While sitting in the emergency waiting room, Roderick seemed to get a little impatient after a longer wait…

"It's been over an hour since we've been sitting here." "What do I have to do to get them to do their jobs? Oh, I get it, I would have to be someone very important in order to get some kind of attention, I probably would had seen him by now." Roderick said in frustration. "Now stop getting yourself worked up honey, it's not helping." Sheila said. "What we should be doing is praying for your father for quick recovery."

Roderick nodded his head in agreement. They bowed their heads first in silence. Roderick began first praying in his mind… (God, please don't let anything happen to my father. If you see that he lives, I will forgive him for letting my mother die, please let him live…Amen.) Sheila continues to rub Roderick's back as he was praying… "You ok baby?" Sheila asked. "Yeah, I guess I'm alright."

"What did you pray for?" "I asked God to spare his life, so that I could forgive him for my mother's accident." "That's good baby." As they continued to comfort one another, the Doctor appeared to tell them the news… "Mr. Jackson?" "Yes, that's me." "Hi, my name is Doctor Mohr, I'm the one along with other medical assistance, who operated on your father." "We've repaired a clogged artery in the last two hours. The operation was a success. However, it does not take him completely out of the woods, for he needs plenty of rest. You may see him now as long as it is brief." The doctor said with a smile.

As he proceeded to walk away Roderick reached to shake his hand to say "Thank you Doctor, you saved his life." "No, thank God, not me! Have a blessed day young man!" Both Sheila and Roderick proceeded anxiously to the "ICU" where his father was resting. Now in "ICU", both Roderick and Sheila were at the bedside of Roderick's father, while a nurse is checking for his vital signs… He looks tired" Sheila said. As she looked over at her father-in-law, she can see how closely Roderick resembles his father very much except one has gray bushy hair with rough looking face. Roderick, on the other hand is bald with no hair and a mustache.

He holds his father's hand while looking at him… "Mr. Jackson, you are welcome to stay the night if you like, as long as you don't disturb your father's rest." "Thank you, nurse!" Roderick said with a smile. "You're welcome." The nurse turned around and headed out the room. "So, what is it that you want to do Rod?" "I guess I'll have to stay tonight." "No, I'll stay tonight you go home." "Besides, you have to work tomorrow, that gives you a chance to take your mind off things." Sheila said. "Are you sure?" "Yes, of course I'm sure." "While you take care of home, I will take care of our father."

Roderick looked over at his father, he went into deep thought as he held his father's hand thinking… (God must had answered my prayers, so I forgive you pops for Mama not being here with us.) He also remembers one of many conversations what his father used to say to him… (Son, I'm not trying to make you do anything that you don't want to do, but at least consider the opportunity of living for God, instead of yourself… But Dad, not everyone can do or be like you! I wasn't made to do what you do… But son, you don't know that until you search your heart and find out what's really there. And besides, I do not have much time left and my hope is that you reconsider and be my next successor…)

Roderick's deep chain of thought now broken by Sheila… "Honey! It's getting late." "Are you going to be ok?" Sheila asked. "Yeah, I'll be alright." "Just lookout for him if you can." Roderick said. "I will…oh, don't forget we have an appointment." Sheila said. "Appointment? What appointment Sheila?" "The realtor, don't you remember?" "Oh yeah, what time again was that?" "5pm sharp if we want to buy this house, our first home." "So, meet me there and don't be late."

"There's a problem with that!" "What's that Rod?" I have to work late until 6pm, so you have to tell them later than 5pm. "Why didn't you tell me this before Roderick!" Sheila said with haste. "Well, I was going to tell you but this happened and of course I forgot." "But Rod, you knew this before all this happened, a whole week ago, so don't use that as an excuse." "Look! Just tell that realtor we had an emergency and we will meet them at 7pm!" Roderick said with irritation in his voice. But the sound of desperation for Roderick to change his schedule, tension began to rise between the both of them... "Look, if you mess this up, I'm going to be upset and disappointed." Sheila said. But Roderick turned around to say "Upset??" "My father just had a stroke and heart attack and you worried about some freak'n appointment with a house that can wait??"

"Woman, that's your problem right there, your priorities are off, so Sheila get your act together and together quick!!" Roderick shouted. "Honey, I didn't mean it that way, I'm sorry." Sheila said with empathy. "Then what in hell was that supposed to mean?" "I tell you what Sheila, get on the phone and tell them what I said, we will meet them at 7pm. So, get your mind right by taking care of my father tonight!

You got that? See you tomorrow!" Roderick leaves irritated. Sheila now feels speechless after the argument, and doesn't know where to pick up the pieces but to turn back to Roderick's father as he sleeps. Hours now has passed with no signs of Roderick's father awakening; Sheila steady looks over him to see for any changes until the door opens from the room where Sheila and her father-in-law is... "Surprise it's me!" Roderick shouted.

Sheila looks up with surprise like a child happy to see their parent. "Hey honey I thought you weren't talking to me for the rest of the night." "Well, you know I couldn't stay mad at you, since you were the one volunteered to stay and watch over dad. Besides, I figured you might need some things to get you through the night like our laptop, so you can get some work done while you are here." "That was very thoughtful of you honey come here." Sheila gets up to hug Roderick and kisses him, but to smell on his breath… "Honey! You've been drinking again?" "Just had a couple of beers to keep my mind off things." Roderick justified. Sheila looked up to him with concerned eyes… "Honey, I know you've been under a lot of stress, so you really should take it easy on the alcohol ok?" Sheila softly said. "Don't worry babe, I'll be alright."

"So, how is dad doing?" Roderick quickly shifted the attention off him to his father. "Dad is doing fine, but he's under heavy sedation, so I don't think he will be waking up anytime soon." "Ok, good then. Roderick replied. "Well, don't want to interrupt anything, so I better get home to rest myself and you rest too my Sheila." Roderick proceeded to move quickly out the door until Sheila grabs him by the arm before he was able to dash out the room… "What's your hurry Rod?" "Are you forgetting something?" Roderick, at first had a blank look on his face, but soon realized that he was still holding on to the computer bag with all of her things… "Oh, my baad, lol!" "No dear, it's my bag, my computer bag, lol" Sheila said. They kissed each other quickly than Roderick leaves. Sheila looking dumfounded not really knowing what's going on with Roderick, begins to set up a corner spot in the room to work while her father-in-law sleeps. As she stationed herself with her chair and table, see proceeds to take the laptop out of bag with other things, "Aww, he remembered my favorite snacks cherry fruit bars." She said with a smile. But when she touched the laptop, it felt warm, so when she lifted the screen it immediately comes on… "How many times do I have to tell him to remember safely shut down my computer when finished!"

"It's bad enough when we got only one computer that works from the last, he broke." Sheila further gets settled by simply resting before she decides to do any work on the computer, but before rest, she sorts out what paperwork she wants to look over in the morning. Once, it was very quiet from the noises of people walking and movement of equipment going from room to room, she suddenly hears voices that she could not recognize before and not knowing where it's coming from. She looked around the room, no one insight. She looked out the room to look both ways of the hall, no one in sight. So, she returns back to the room to say "I must be tired because I'm now hearing voices, lol" Sheila sits down in her corner area and relieves a sigh, but before she could close her eyes for a moment of rest, comes the noise again.

So, Sheila sits up again with alertness to look around the room again, the noises she now hears have more clarity in sound… "It sounds like someone's moaning in pain." She now turns to her laptop and opens it to discover a page Roderick never closed out or forgotten… "What? What in the hell is this?" Sheila tried to determine exactly what she was looking at, but couldn't because the light of the room overshadowed the dense light of the laptop screen, but was able enough to determine the exact noises she heard earlier… "It looks like porn!" "Why would Roderick be looking at porn?" As she continued to investigate the page, her fear began to rise as her anger of what's next she would find. Trying to keep her composure, realizing that she's in a public hospital room with her father-in-law, fighting rage in her emotions she continues to look deeper into the page website Roderick left open "It looks like a lot of naked people having orgies or something from men making out with men, and men making it out with women, and women making it out with other women. Can't tell exactly." After this sudden discovery of what Roderick does in the dark, Sheila sits back in her chair in amazement and troubled at what she just seen by rubbing her head, then began to question in her mind (I thought I really knew Roderick, we went to the same high school together and never knew he had this secret hidden in him.)

As she sat trying to put the pieces together… "Cough, cough!" Sheila heard coughs coming from her father-in-law now quickly exits the page that was left from Roderick and closes the laptop screen so no one else could see what was discovered… "Cough, cough!" Sheila looked over at her father-in-law to rush to his aid to say… "It's ok father, just take it easy." "Cough, who is that?" "It's me Sheila dad." "Sheila?" "Cough, is that you?" He said with a screeching broken voice. "Yes father, it's me, just rest now." "Where am I?" He asked. "Don't worry, you are safe here with me, just rest." Sheila said with comfort. She rubbed her father's head and kissed it. He looked up at Sheila, comforted by her words, like a child ready to go to sleep after a bed story told by his parent, without a blink as he stared at Sheila, fell immediately back to sleep from the medication he was under. Sheila returns back to her area to open up the laptop to quickly erase any search history of this discovery and to avoid any computer viruses it could had surfaced. As Sheila sat to think what to say and do to Roderick for looking at porn without her consent, she quickly rationalizes and justify his act to say… "All men look at porn, so why should I be tripping over it now." "I forgive him for now, but I won't forget!" She moved on to proceed with her work.

CHAPTER 8

Hidden Enemy –
Date to Bombshell

IT HAS BEEN SEVERAL DAYS SINCE I HEARD FROM Darryl after our deep hours of conversation over the phone, I took liberty to call and strike conversation since it was probably my turn to call… "Ring, ring" "Hello?" "Hey what's up?" "Wow look at that!" "Ms. Lady called me for a change!" "What gave me the honor of you calling, lol!" "Darryl said. "Stop trying to be funny Darryl, lol!" "Now that I have you on the phone, it was on my mind to call and ask if you and Sabrina would like to go out tonight on a date and a movie?"

"Technically Darryl, it wouldn't be called a date since you are inviting my daughter Sabrina." "Well, I say it's a date because it's Friday night, and I just got paid, and the weather is a bombshell where it's not too hot but a breeze we all can share, and besides, who wrote the definition on date anyway? If you really want to get technical, the word "date" means object or event, now if you want to determine more in debts of the word, it can be changed to a verb called dating which entails more than just the object or event, but it looks for commitment…" "Ok, ok, Mr. Professor of Vocabulary, lol" (What he didn't know, is that he turned me on down there if you know what I mean… I love a man who is intelligent and can stimulate my mind that triggers sometimes something else, but men on an average wouldn't know that because they often think with their other head).

"So, tonight you say?" "Ok, what's playing tonight?" "This new movie that just came out called "AVATAR" it premieres tonight which is why I thought it would be nice if we all get out." "Besides, it is a chance for me to meet the little princess Sabrina." "Good! What time does the movie start Darryl?" "It starts at 9pm so, I'll pick you up around 7:30pm to assure that we have good parking." "That works out fine Darryl." "We will be ready by the time you get here." I confirmed. Just as we hang up, another call followed right behind it… "Yes baby, did you forget something?" I hear a pause but no reply, so I asked again… "Darryl, you hear me?" "No, this is not Darryl." "Who is this?" "Wow! You still sound good Cheryl and I must say I miss hearing that sexy voice of yours, this is Michael." Soon as I heard his voice and name, my heart began to pound faster from the embarrassment, not expecting to hear from him ever again.

"Ok Michael, what is it that you want?" "Are you calling to tell me that you decided to be man enough about your responsibilities?" "No Cheryl!" "But since you want to bring that up, I'm working on it and won't run anymore." "In fact, I'm a changed man who gave his life to God, and going to Church regularly; working to do better while time is short and don't know how much time is left. But for now, I want to see Sabrina in the near future if that's ok with you." "That's great to hear about your new venture in life, but seeing Sabrina anytime soon, I'm not sure if that's a good idea." "What do you mean by that Cheryl?" "Sabrina is my daughter and responsibility." He said. "You lost that right when you left your family for what you did!" "I understand how you feel Cheryl and I'm not here to defend my actions, I'm telling you however, I do own the right to see my daughter, you didn't bring her into this life by yourself!" (He pauses) "Ok, ok, let me calm down a bit, if you must know, I have a new job as a senior mechanic in a well-known shop!" "You will be receiving some funds for my daughter soon." Michael said.

"Michael, it's not about me which is what you don't understand, it's about Sabrina, if she wants to see you or have you in her life." I said. "Well, don't worry about that, I will see my daughter and don't think whatever you say to her, can stop me from seeing my child, especially when I will be paying dues." Michael said. "Cheryl, if necessary, I will take this to court for joint custody if I have to…" "Ok Michael!!" I shouted to interrupt his thoughts…

"I'm not going to argue with you about this! If anyone should be mad is me for what you did to me and Sabrina, so please, don't go there with me!!" I shouted. "Ok, ok Cheryl calm down, I didn't call you for all of this; I called to tell you something else…" (But before Michael was able to tell me or say the next thing the doorbell rings…) "Michael sorry, I must go, I will call you back!"

I hang up the phone quickly to rush to the door to my surprise… "Hello, hello, hello!" "Darryl?" "I thought we…" He grabs me into his arms and gave me the biggest kiss of my life that made me forget the call from Michael for a moment… "Honey, I thought we agreed…" Darryl pulls out 23 roses in a vase and 1 single vase he held behind his back "Here you go baby and one for the princess!" "Thank you, baby, you didn't have to go through all that trouble for us." "Baby, you no trouble to me." (Oh I see what Kim was talking about now, a man say the right thing at the most opportune time, we ready to give up the panties…but not today, maybe tomorrow if he say the right thing again, because tonight, we got a movie to go to, lol) "I thought we had agreed a time around 7:30-7:45pm to pick us up?" "Well, you know I can't stay away from you too long so, surprise still! I'm here!" "Did I catch you at a bad time?" "No, no, come on inside baby."

Darryl comes inside with a bag in addition to the roses in his hand and goes straight to the kitchen to pull two glasses from my cabinet… "Darryl, what are you doing?" "What does it look like?" "Got this bottle of wine that's cold and ready to pop. It's chardonnay, one of the finest wines on the market. I figured that we could enjoy a glass or two before Sabrina gets home from school and perhaps enjoy some quality time together, since we haven't seen each other in a while." "Is that ok with you?" "So, in other words Darryl, you were feeling kinda horny and you knew Sabrina wouldn't be home in another hour or so, and to see if I was up to fulfilling your sexual quest, right?"

The look on his face was of shock that I was able to read his mind and how he worked on a mission to see if it was possible. I give him credit for at least trying…Now Darryl feeling guilty after what he said, he had that look if someone broke his heart with his lip poked out expecting the worse. I picked up my glass of wine that he poured for me and sipped a couple of drinks, I looked at the clock, to see what time we had left, then I looked into his eyes to see what he was thinking and to say next. "You can get ready earlier or we can play a card game of spades or even casino, or…" "Ok, let's go for it!" I said. "Ok, let me pull out the cards, which game you wanna play? Casino, spades, or…" "Romper room Darryl." "I don't know that game baby you might have to show me this one." Darryl said. "Don't worry, I'll show you how this game is played." I take him to my room, he soon figured it out what's about to go down.

Later that night, the three of us enjoyed the night watching the premier movie and a dinner at "TGIF" restaurant. It lasted all the way until midnight. That Monday while at work, after the weekend was over, Darryl leaves a beautiful message saying how much he enjoyed the time with me and Sabrina. He also informs me that his job will be doing annual mandatory physical check-up and must go for his appointment and will call me later. Just that message it put me in a blissful mood at work while dealing with both conceited nurses who think they are God's gift on earth, while the Doctors feel they have all the solutions to world's mayhem of problems that constantly arises in the emergency rooms.

When I think about it, I'm glad to be able to forget about my problems by focusing on other people's problems. But sometimes that don't always work, because just as soon as I would feel good after one message from Darryl, here comes someone who tries to steal my joy… "Ugh, Michael leaves another text message!" "Why can't he just leave me alone!" I checked the message from Michael saying "Cheryl you never called me back like you said you would. Last I remembered, you said you will call back and never did." "Now Cheryl, you've always been a woman of your word, please call back, I have something to tell you." It totally slipped my mind to call him back for obvious reasons… I can't imagine what's so important that can't just leave on the message, for me to call to talk live. It might be that he really hired a lawyer for joint child custody of Sabrina, or child support.

I must hurry get back to work before someone say something about me on the phone… (phone rings) "Spoke to soon, lol!" "Hello" "Hey Cheryl, it's me Kim!" "What's going on Girl?" "You at work today? I didn't see you yet." Kim asked. "Yes, I am but today I'm working on the northside of the hall." "Oh, ok is everything alright?" "You don't sound too good." "Did Darryl make you mad?" "No Girl, it's Michael again." "What about Michael?" "I know you ain't thinking…" "No Girl, I'm not!" "It's that I can't seemed to focus on my job today without Michael leaving constant messages for me to call him back to talk about something he doesn't want to leave in a message." "I can't figure it out." "Do you have any Ideas what it might be?" Kim asked. "No, I don't. The only thing I can come up with is he's possibly pursuing legal assistants getting joint custody that I don't want him to have. He also mentioned he has a job now and wants to be part of Sabrina's life." "Well that's good!" "You should be happy about that, right?" Kim asked. "I know Girl, but he also said he had something else important to tell me, but never wants to leave it on the message." "Well, If I were you, I would stop worrying about it; just call him back to see what he's talking about or wait until he calls again." "Ok Girl, maybe you're right!" "I'll call him later." "Good for you." "Well, I must get back to work." "I'll talk you soon Kim!"

"Ok Cheryl have a good day, bye!" I can always count on Kim when I feel down to bring me back up. Love that Girl! Months past and weeks gone by, things seemed to be coming together for me as I finally found love again in my life, Darryl who has made me feel like more than woman that I ever would be, Sabrina looks up to him like a child would with her father, the job is going well, and I haven't yet heard back from Michael, so all is good. I take off from work for much needed rest and spring cleaning from the crazy weather we've been having with tremendous rain lately, this was the opportunity to get it done until, "knock, knock!" "Who's knocking at my door before 12 noon?" I looked outside of the window to see without him seeing me, and to my surprise… "Darryl?" "What's he's doing here?" I quickly open the door… "Hey Darryl, what's going on?" "I wasn't expecting you honey."

As I'm talking, I've noticed on Darryl's face it wasn't the same excited face he would have every time he would show up to my house. It was obvious that something was wrong because the look he had was a grin on his face with troubled look as though he may had lost his job or someone, he really cared for... "What's wrong Darryl?" "Come in!" Silently, Darryl comes in with his head bowed down but with high emotions I never seen before. "Talk to me Darryl, you are scaring me!" I'm having a feeling of fear and insecurity of what in Darryl's mind because of the anger I sense from him.

So, the silence finally broke by him asking me a question "How long has it been since we've been together?" "I don't know, maybe six months or more, why you ask?" As Darryl paced the floor rubbing his face with one hand and the other in his pants pocket, he responds by saying... "I received my medical exam results today thinking I was getting a raise from my over-due performance appraisal, and it's not good." He said with sternness in his voice. I tried to calm him down by going to him by rubbing his chest while holding his arm... "What do you mean not good Darryl?" "I mean this thing here can jeopardize my whole career with this company." He said with panic in his voice. "What do you mean by that Darryl?" "You're not being specific, tell me!" He looked at me as though I did something terribly wrong, looking down at the floor as he continued to pace and look at me in discuss... "Tell me the truth Cheryl, are you having an affair or seeing someone else?" "Are you keeping secrets from me!!" Darryl shouted.

Oh, the thought that raced my mind was (how dare this boy accuse me of cheating) "Answer me Cheryl are you seeing someone else!!" "Don't come to my house demanding a damn thing from me and to accuse me of something I'm not doing!!" "You don't own the right to come in my house with that attitude!!" "First of all Darryl, what right do you have to shout at me like I'm some child!!" "Secondly, you know damn well I haven't been with anyone else!! I thought you knew me a little better than that coming at me with that stupid question!!"

"Well, that same stupid question gave me the stupid results from my physical exam and test of a stupid report I have HIV!! He shouted. My face dropped after hearing Darryl's claim and report… "You have what?" "HIV!!" "So, what's really going on Darryl?" "What do you mean by that Cheryl?" "You really expect me to believe that I gave you HIV when you really got it from elsewhere while at work driving your trucks?" "How low can you really get Darryl?" "I thought you really loved me!" "Wait a minute don't try to change this all-around Cheryl…" "Don't try to put it on me Darryl!!" I interrupted him. "It's really a bad trick Darryl and I'm not fooled at all by it!" "I knew it was a bad idea of getting involved with a truck driver!!" I shouted.

I took steps back to get away from him because at that moment I didn't want to be touched. With mixed emotions, I was trying to catch my composure, but before I can think the next thing to say to him, it suddenly registered in my mind that "Wait a minute, just wait a minute!! You gave me HIV and tried to blame me given to you!!" "Oh Darryl, how could you possibly stoop that low, I thought you were better than that.!!" Darryl now feeling puzzled. "What are you talking about Cheryl?" "You know what I'm talking about! You gave me the virus and didn't want me to find out about it."

"But because your job made you get tested, and you couldn't hide it any longer but to find someone else to blame." "You came here thinking I would fall for something stupid like that by taking the fall for your cheating, when really you slept with another trash woman that gave it to you!!" Darryl looks back at me with a state of confusion and disbelief of what he was hearing. But before he could react to what I just said, emotions burst out state of disbelief what is happening to me, I couldn't control the tears that began to flow knowing that my life of happiness, and peace I regained back, now interrupted by pain and scars that was once healed, now again re-opened. Darryl tried to rush to me with aid to grab my arm to say… "I didn't do anything to harm this relationship!" "I've never contracted STD until now after meeting you." "So, you tell me who's the blame?"

Instead of him trying to help my tears from flowing, he dared to say that to me. "What I can't believe Darryl, is we're having this conversation!" "Let go of my arm Darryl!" "You still have the nerve, with no remorse, to assume I'm the one who has STD and cheated on you, I mean really Darryl?" "You must think I'm some cheap dirty hoe or something, and if so, you are the sorriest guy I ever met!" "Even my ex-husband would have better sense to man up to his own mistakes unlike you!" "You mean your gay husband?" Darryl said with sarcasm in his voice. "You know what

Darryl, it's time for you to leave and to get out of my life!" Darryl's look on his face was anger in his eyes, but also hurt… "Get out Darryl I mean it!!" I opened the door while mascara still running down my face from the flood of tears.

As he was leaving out the door, he slowly looks back at me with both sorrow and hurt in his eyes, but with no words to say… I slammed the door closed before he could say another word. As I slowly peaked out the window to watch him leave, I can see him confused and troubled not able to get the key in his ignition quick enough before I can see him burst into tears himself, then he drove off. I turned away from the window to feel the great burden on my chest, the pain of now once getting over Michael, has added another pain of grief, Darryl. I don't know how much more can I take. Life isn't fair! Thank you, Darryl for screwing my life all over again!

CHAPTER 9

Who's fooling Who? – House Hunting

THE NEXT DAY WHILE RODERICK IS AT WORK… "RING, Ring!" Roderick's cell phone rings "Hello!" "Hey Rod it's me, how soon will you be getting off work today?" Sheila asked. "First off, good afternoon to you!" "And how are you and Pops doing?"

Roderick asked. "He's fine and awake." "He asked about you, but I told him you are at work, but was here yesterday while he slept." "Good looking out Sheila!" "So, what time Rod?" "Look, quit your worrying, I told you that I will be there at 7pm." "Did you call the realtor to reschedule Sheila?"

There was a sudden pause from Sheila, between thinking what she discovered on the computer and dealing with less sleep... "Did you hear me Sheila?" "What?" "What did you ask me Rod?" "I ask you did you call the realtor to reschedule the 5pm appointment to 7pm?" Sheila suddenly remembered that it slipped her mind to call and hurried off the phone... "Call you back Rod, bye!" So, Sheila was successfully able to immediately reschedule the appointment to see the house at 7pm with the realtor with a sigh of relief, but still with pessimism and insecurity of going forth with a purchase of a new home with Roderick, knowing he has issues of infidelity online porn on her computer, not knowing if he has interest to take it further with some other woman in person.

As she sat watching the nurse attend her father-in-law, she thinks further in her mind to say (Roderick got some issues and doing something I don't like... But then, I might be overreacting and need to stay focused on helping his father back to health and to get our first home.) Roderick, while at work... "Roderick! We have a customer complaint about their shipment they received. He's saying the product we sent was defected and is not running properly." "What should we do?" Theresa, his employee asked. "Re-issue a new computer that's been fully tested and request the old back immediately." Roderick ordered. "No problem."

"Hey by the way, I've been meaning to ask you the longest time, what made you decide this career over a basketball career since your height fits the occasion?" Theresa asked. "Well, you may not know this, but I had a terrible car accident that messed up my legs and broke both of my knee caps and almost couldn't walk again." Theresa stood back from Roderick with an embarrassed look on her face not knowing... "I'm so sorry Mr. Roderick, I was really paying you a compliment, I didn't know..." "It's ok Theresa, many people have asked me the same question, lol" "I'm good and over it, I have a good career now and life is looking good for me now." "But nice try kissing up to the boss though, I have to give you that credit, lol"

"Ok, you got me Mr. Roderick, I guess I can kiss that request for raise for another time, lol" "Lol, probably so Theresa, lol!" "Hey Theresa which reminds me, I have to leave early today to take care some business, I need you to hold it down while I'm out." "It's my wedding anniversary next week, and I need to prepare for it." "Congratulations Mr. Roderick!" "Going anywhere special with your wife?" "Yes, we're going to Las Vegas to stay at the "Mirage Hotel" for our anniversary." "Wow!! That sounds really nice!" Theresa said with excitement in her voice. (Ring, ring) "Hold on Theresa this is my wife calling, shhh." "Hello!" Roderick reclines back into his chair while looking over at Theresa as she bends over to reach for a stapler over his desk showing a little cleavage, he could not help but to stare without her noticing him looking while listening to Sheila, his wife discussing arrangements for the appointment with the realtor… "Good baby!" "I'll be there at 7pm!" (click)

"Well, it looks like I have a lot to do tonight." "Oh really Mr. Roderick?" "I'm about to purchase my first home and then head out for vacation with the wifey!" "What more can I ask for!" Roderick said smilingly as he leans back in his chair with both hands back of his head feeling a sense of achievement. "That's wonderful news Sir!" "I'm sure your wife will love it!" "Well, I must be leaving now, hopefully you guys have everything under control for the rest of the day." "Take care the rest of these invoices for me ok Theresa!" "Sure, I can do that! Have fun ok!" Roderick looks at the innocence of Theresa with her long hair and sexy body to say to himself (Boy, I wish I could had met you before I met my wife, I could go for a Latina woman right about now…) Roderick hurried to grab his bag and coat before his lust thoughts hold him hostage for what he needs to do and says… "See you all later!"

As he leaves the building to go to his car, he opens the door to sit down to slowly start the ignition. But before he could put the car in gear, his thoughts went back to Sheila to think to himself (Sheila didn't seem happy with all the news changing the time or something. It sounded sad now I think about it. Maybe the stress of my Father's health and her staying back and forth from home to the hospital is taking a toll on her.) His thoughts continued… (Maybe I need to check in with Pops, to see how he's doing.) Roderick picks up his cellphone to begin calling the hospital where his Father is staying… "Hello, thank you for call Chicago Medical how can we help you?" "Hello, I wish to speak to a patient by the name of Mr. Palmer Jackson in "ICU" "One moment please." As Roderick waited for a response from the nurse, as he was now driving while on the phone, he carefully stayed attentive to his surroundings, thinking subconsciously of what happened tragically to his mother… "Hello!" "Who are you waiting for?" The nurse asked. "I'm waiting to hear from Mr. Palmer Jackson, my father, who was admitted over a week ago." "Yes, Mr. Jackson is still here and he's now resting and cannot be disturbed." The nurse said. "Do you know if my wife Sheila Jackson is still there?" "No sir, she's not here." "Do you know when she left?" "No sir, I don't." The nurse responded. "Thank you!" Roderick hung up the phone as he continued to drive headed out to the appointment with the realtor.

Now at the property seeking to purchase, Sheila now arrives greeted by the realtor waiting just outside the door… "Hello Sheila, nice to speak with you again now in person! Katie the realtor said with excitement. "Hi Katie, nice to meet you too!" "Where's your husband?" "Oh, he should be here soon!" "That's great!" "It's better that I have both of you here, so that you two can agree together on this house." Katie said. Before Sheila could respond to that comment, nerves of intensity were building up at first because Roderick was 10 minutes late… "Well look at that! Here he is now pulling up the driveway." Sheila said. As Roderick parked to turn the ignition off, he looked over at Sheila, to determine the mood she might be in whether it be happy genuinely or pretended, he gets out of the car to go greet her… "Hey baby I'm here, am I late?" Sheila looked at him not knowing how to answer that but kept her composure to say… "No dear, just glad you made it, now let's go meet Katie." Sheila now grabs Roderick's arm to go meet the realtor… "Rod, this is Katie our Realtor." "Hello Mr. Jackson! It's a pleasure to meet you as my potential new homeowners!" She said with excitement.

As Roderick extends his hand to shake her hand, he suddenly begins to thinks to himself… (Man she looks exactly like that Asian lady from the show "House Hunters" … "Now, you two, let's go inside to tour your potential new home!" Katie said. As the realtor began to escort both Sheila and Roderick inside, Katie couldn't help to notice Roderick and say… "Boy Mr. Jackson, I most certainly hope this house can accommodate your height, lol" "I'm sure that the house my wife picked out will do just fine." Both now Sheila and Roderick toured the 2,800 sq. ft. house with 3 bedrooms and 2 ½ baths home inside and out with astound approval… "It has all the upgrades included, hard wood cherry floors, steel stain appliances, granite kitchen tops, his and hers walk in closets, and fireplaces both in the family room and master bedroom, and two car garage." Katie said. "When was this house build and how much is the asking price again?" Roderick asked. "It's about a year old, build in 2008, and the asking price is $330,000 or best offer since the market for housing has crashed and it became the buyer's market." Katie said.

Roderick looked back at Sheila now that the tour was almost over to ask… "what do you think? You like it?" Sheila looked back at him to say… "Yes, honey but first, let's be smart about this, I want to see if the asking price can be lowered." "Smart baby, real smart." As they both were discussing their decision whether to purchase or not, Katie looks over at them with confidence they will proceed with house… "Ok Katie, this is what we decided, we want to proceed but we also want to see if we can make an offer of $300,000 instead of asking price." Sheila said. After she said that, both Roderick and Katie were surprised at the offer not knowing she would make such an offer at less price. "Well, here's what I can do, since this is a recent foreclosure, and the previous owner didn't stay for long, let's see what the bank says." "However, I must say I admire the bargaining techniques you have Sheila! Lol!" "Well, I can't let my business degree go to waste, so I must use it when needed lol!" Sheila said. Sheila holds Roderick's hand tightly and looked at him to say "I want this house Roderick so make sure we get it!" "Gotcha baby!" "I'm going to say in confidence that this will be your new home." "I'm sure with your good credit that was last checked, it would not be a problem for the bank to move forward." "Congratulations! Your house hunting is over!" Katie said with confidence. "Tomorrow, I will make some calls and get the necessary paperwork prepared for you both." "I'm sure escrow won't last as long as average time of wait, so I'm will assume that you two will be owners in no time soon." Katie said with assuredness.

Roderick looks over at Sheila and Katie before leaving to say… "Just one more thing Katie. We won't be here next week in case things go well, because I'm taking my wife on a trip to Las Vegas for our Wedding Anniversary!" "That's a great surprise! Congratulations!!" Sheila's looks on her face was a look of surprise going to Disneyland… With excitement, overwhelmed with the good news, Sheila for the moment forgets whatever happened in her discovery to thank Roderick with a big kiss. "By the way you two, by the time you return, the house will be waiting and ready for you. Have a wonderful trip and I'll see you soon!" So, Katie gets into her car then leaves the premises with the sense of accomplishment, another home sold in her books. "Honey, I want to really thank you for making my day!" "You are welcome baby!" "You deserve the best; we deserve the best! We've worked hard for this day to come." After that comment he made to Sheila, he began to notice on her face that she wasn't totally sold on what he just said. As she walked back to her car he asked. "Are you ok honey?" "You don't seem to be excited anymore now that Katie is gone." "Is there anything I need to know?" Sheila looked back at Roderick with a blank look so say… "No dear remember, you made my day!" "I'm going back to the hospital to check on your father, and to run to the store to get a couple of things, make sure that you check in with me when I get there to the hospital." Sheila said. "You sure about that?" Roderick asked. "I'll be ok, see you at home."

But before she was able to get into the car, Roderick again ask… "Are you sure you ok, I know it's been a toll on you looking after my father at the hospital. I just want to make sure that you are ok and…" "Roderick! Stop asking me the same repeated questions over and over! Now irritated, Sheila said. "Ok, ok just asking." "I'll see you later Roderick." Sheila gets into her car, starts the ignition, and drives off without even looking back at Roderick. But Roderick, who begins to start his ignition as he's now in the car thinks to himself (I was going to ask her out to dinner, but I guess I'll head on to the crib, since it seems like she's in one of those moods.) Before driving off, Roderick begins to shift gears of what he thinks to do… (I probably need to check on Pops, even though I haven't truly forgiven him for mama's death, by calling the hospital again, to see how he's doing…)

He calls the hospital while driving… "Hello, thank you for calling Chicago Medical may I help you?" "Yes, I'm calling for Mr. Palmer Jackson please!" "What's your relationship to this patient Sir?" "I'm his son, Roderick Jackson." "Hold on please while I transfer you…" "Hello!" "Pops?" "It's me Roderick!" He said with excitement in his voice. "Son! How are you?" "I should be asking you that Pops, how are you doing?" "I'm doing much better son, thanks for asking." "You sound good Pops, I'm glad you are doing better." "Why haven't you visit me yet?"

"Oh, Pops I've been there several times, but you were sleep every time, and the nurses didn't want me to bother you like that." Roderick justified. "I've seen Sheila here many of times, and I was glad to see some family here in my time of need." His Father said. "In fact, Sheila should be on her way back to see you." "I had to take care of the home and job while she had more time to be with you is why I can't be there often." "I understand son." "Are you ok Pops?" "Cough, cough!" "I'm ok son, it was a close one they tell me." "But the doctor says I'll be fine in a week or two, but for me to continue to get much needed rest." "Wait a minute son, the nurse is waving at me…ok nurse, I will…" "Son, the nurse is telling me I must go now, we talk later." "Wait Pops! Before you go, I must tell you what happened today." "What's that son?" "It looks like things are coming together for Sheila and I." "What do you mean son?" "We're in the process of buying our first home…"

"That's good son! Glad to hear that!!" "Cough, cough!" "God is blessing you and Sheila with a home of your own." "Before I forget son, Happy anniversary to you and Sheila!" "Wow Pops! I didn't think you would remember that!" "Well, I didn't but your wife was happy to remind me, lol" "Awesome Pops!" "We hope to close on the house after we return from vacation, I didn't tell you, but I'm also taking Sheila to Las Vegas for a week, will you be ok while we're gone? Roderick asked. "Wow son that great to hear!" "I think I'll be fine, I believe they are confident now to move me out of "ICU" to a regular room, so I'll be fine." "That's great Pops!" "I'm sure that your mother was here, she would be very proud of you and Sheila…"

After his father made that comment, Roderick began to think back the pain and tragic death of his mother in that car accident… "Son, are you there?" "I'm here Pops." "Just caught a tear running down my face in remembrance of mom." "Well, just as I told you before, don't blame yourself for your mother's accident. It wasn't your fault that she's not here." "I know Pops, but I can't help it, (Truly, I blame you dad!) I guess I'll never get over it…" "I just wished that she was here to celebrate both Sheila and I's success." "It still hurts Pops, and I still feel it's my fault that it all happened." "Well Son, you can't continue this life blaming yourself, otherwise you will never a peace of mind." "Besides, if anything your mother would want from you now is go on strong leaving the past behind you." "Son, the nurse is waving at me again to hang up." "Ok Pops, I'll let you go."

But before Roderick was able to hang up the phone, his father would ask…" Son, one more thing, are you reading your bible? (I've should had known this was coming…) Roderick thought back to himself. "Umm, Pops I really didn't have the time because of work and you now being sick, and now getting ready to purchase our first new home, but I will soon try when both Sheila and I get back from vacation, promise." Roderick justified. "Now Son, as I told you before, a family that prays together, stays together." "So, don't slack any further." "Gotcha Pops – I here you." "Now Son, I'm depending on you in case I would pass on to glory. I would like for my only son to take over when the church for me."

"Now Pops, I thought you had to get off the phone, first thing is first, obey the nurse Pops!" Roderick said irritated by the gesture of his Father. "Yes, you are right son, I must go." "Ok Pops, have a good night we will see you when we get back, I love you." "I love you too son, bye." Roderick begins to say to himself… (Man, that was a long conversation I had with Pops! He needs to stop looking at me to take his church, my heart is not in it and I don't want it. Besides there are plenty people in his church that are well capable of taking over instead of me. Sorry Pops, won't happen promise you that! Although I forgave you temporarily for mom's death, and can't help but not forget you had a role in it.

Especially now that mom couldn't be here to see my life's success, forget about it Pops, forget about it!) "I gotta hurry home before Sheila, so I can chill and mellow out from all this mess to forget my problems, without Sheila trip' pin and my father beating over my head about something he wants, and forgetting why my mother isn't here." Roderick soon arrived back to their apartment and notice the empty spot where Sheila normally would park her car… "Cool!!" Sheila ain't home yet." Now inside their apartment, Roderick prepares to settle down with two cold beers out the fridge… "Man! There's only two beers left!" "I'll call Sheila to pick me up some since she's going to the store anyway after visiting Pops before she come home… (Ring, ring, ring, ring…) Sheila doesn't pick up but her voice message starts… "Hey, hey babe it's me, while at the store, could you pick up a six pack for me, the same high gravity beers. Thanks!"

Roderick now heads to the bedroom computer that Sheila left behind on the bed. He looks at the time on the clock that now read "It's 8:30pm, which means she should be at the hospital by now and won't be back for another hour or two…" He said out loud. While reclined back on their king size bed, he opens his first can of gravity beer and took a big gulp, in hopes to feel a quick high from it. He turned his attention to the TV, by turning up the volume to catch the latest news… "In recent studies, there has been another murder that had something to deal with Craigslist our Reporter reports… "That's correct Jim, and we have details on that information in the next hour, but I must warn you that the details of this story are horrific…"

"Wow! What's the world coming too?" Roderick said out loud. While sitting and tumbling over the TV remote what to watch next, Roderick took another big gulp of his beer that soon made him feel totally relaxed, and some point, his muscles throughout his whole body felt stationary as though he was paralyzed for a moment, then quickly remembers the Craigslist listings, that probably changed his life forever… "Craigslist!" "What's that all about?" "I've heard a little about it but never this magnitude from the news." Roderick gets the computer Sheila left behind on the bed and begins to open it and to search the web for "Craigslist" … "Ahh, there it is…"

After working on the first can of beer now empty, begins on the second can of gravity beer, Roderick became sexually aroused at the thought of looking at women on Craigslist and to see if they would have pictures possibly of naked of them. So now he's in the Craigslist, not knowing where to look, he just picks "Personal Classifieds" "Hmm, what's this about…" He clicks on "WW" "what does this mean?" He asked himself. He clicks on it to discover… "Oh man!" "They got more women on here than I can bargain for…" Now halfway through his second and last gravity beer, he reached to take another big gulp of that can, but noticed that He's becoming too relaxed and getting sleepy, but still his curiosity is keeping him going. From the heaviness of his eyes being tired, his vision becomes impaired, but still able to see, with a strong desire to be satisfied by his curiosity.

As he continues to surf the net in "WW", his searches met his approval of saying… "Man!" "The women on women ain't no joke!" As Roderick continued with his quest, he now saw one site he liked… "She looks good, and that one looks good, and that one girl got backs!!" As he scrolled down on last page visit, he notices a message that says… "No man needs apply" "What?" "No man needs apply?" "That's messed up for real!" "And she got the nerve to put it in bold letters – that's crazy!"

Now irritated after many more that read the same of women he liked, he decided to try another site but still under "Personal Classifieds" He clicks now "WM" … "Hmm, let me see… "Is she for real?" To his dismay, he couldn't find a woman on this site that he would like. "Nope! Keep moving, not this page, next, is this girl really serious? What is she wearing? It looks like she's wearing a thong but it's covered in all that fat, oh well, she needs loving too, lol" Finally, after that disappointment, he takes another big gulp of the remaining beer he had left, but realized he could barely keep his eyes open from now being drunk, wasted from the high gravity beers, but he wasn't done, his drive for satisfaction outweighed his impaired vision, he continued his search… "I'm not getting anywhere with this site!" "Let me try going back to the "WW" I'm sure one of them be willing to holla at me…"

He now has left previous website to venture other potentials until he landed on this… "Now that's what I'm talk'n about right here!" "She looks hella good, yeah!" He continues to scroll on site he's now in to view others that got him excited and more alert. While steady searching, he runs into this one ad… "Bingo!!" "She's hella fine!!" "A knockout body that just won't stop!!" "Reminds me of a famous rapper Nikki something, can't remember her last name, I think I'm wasted now, lol!" He talks out loud to himself. "This one looks young mixed with Asian and Black, some of the finest mixes I like." "Her eyes that looks Asian, makes me wanna scream!" Roderick now stuck on this page and doesn't pursue to any other pages, memorized by this person, he now studies the ad, and begins to read what it says… "Looking for tall handsome man who likes Oral" When Roderick read that, all he could think of what Sheila, his wife doesn't like to do. As Roderick pondered to answer the add, his first thought was "This wouldn't be cheating, right?" "It's not like I'm having sex or anything…" But then he also thought… "What if it is cheating?" "I made an oath man, so I shouldn't be looking at this thinking to go forward with it, besides I have too much to lose if I do this." Roderick, now tries to rationalize his thoughts to say… "I'm just curious really how she sounds and if this Girl really would answer my ad." "If she does, so what. I'm just going to play with it to see how far it will go, but I won't fall for it." "It's cool." "I'm drunk and probably won't remember anything, lol" Roderick justified.

While Roderick continues to study this one page, and hasn't left it to see any other, he tested his guts by clicking on the ad and responded. Suddenly he hears noises… (The door slammed from coming inside the apartment) "Oh no! It's Sheila!" Roderick quickly clicks off the website and Craigslist, and closes it completely now shuts computer down, to rush greet Sheila. "Hey Baby!!" Roderick shouted. "Hey honey, what's up?" Sheila said inquisitively. "Nothing honey, just been watching the tube while chilling on the bed." "Yeah, I'm sure Roderick."

For a minute, Roderick thought he was busted, suspecting Sheila must had knew and was privately watching him… "Then why are you breathing so hard and sweating?" "Just hot baby, it's a little hot in here!" "Yeah, and drinking too." Sheila said in discus. "Ok honey you got me, lol." "Just celebrating how things are going for us over a can a beer, and when I heard you coming in, I assume you may have groceries in the car waiting to be carried." "Did you get my message?" Roderick asked. "Yes, I got it and I tried calling you back, but you didn't answer, so I hope this is what you ask for! Sheila said with a smile. Roderick, with a sigh of relief, he got away with what he feared at the moment, to look in the grocery bags to find the beers he requested. "Yep, Good job baby!!" "Sorry Sheila, I must had left my phone in my pants pocket what I wore earlier today or something." Roderick notices how tired Sheila is with slow movement of the groceries she had in her hand pulling it out one by one with slow movement… "Honey, why don't I get the rest of the groceries while you get settled. It's been a long day for both of us…" Sheila looked up to him in agreement, and a smile… "Thank you honey, I'll take you up on that!" Sheila rubs his smooth face, and walks off… Roderick now rushes to her car to get any remaining groceries while thinking to himself… (Man! I pulled that off smooth, but I must be tripp'n!" "I almost got busted looking at something that never will happen." "What if Sheila would had busted be?" "Glad she didn't, won't happen again!" Just after coming to his senses, soon another thought comes… "But that other Girl was sho'nuff fine!" "Enough me, over with!"

CHAPTER 10

Hidden Enemy – Clinic Visit

JUST AFTER DARRYL LEFT, I TRIED WIPING THE TEARS from my eyes, but didn't have the strength to even raise my arm to do it, after all that has happened. All Darryl did was rehash old wounds that now makes me feel I just can't trust another man, let alone for him to ever come into my life. What's left of my heart to love is now for Sabrina, so she doesn't become damaged goods as I have from bitterness and resentment. The only person that possibly could understand what I'm going through is Kim…

In fact, let me call her because if there was a time, I needed a girlfriend to hear me, is now! (Ring, Ring, Ring…) "Ugh Kim, pick up the phone!" (Ring, ring, ring…) "Great! Her voicemail…!" I wiped the tears from my eyes after finding strength in attempt to talk to someone like my best friend… "Hey Girl it's me Cheryl, I need you to call me back! It's an emergency, call me back!" I said tearfully. As soon as I dropped literally the phone in discus, the phone rings, and it's Kim… "Hello!" I said with tears. "Hey Cheryl I got your message, you don't sound good, what's wrong Girl?" "Darryl and I broke up!!" I said broken heartedly. "Hold on Cheryl, let me get somewhere so that everyone not in this conversation, hold on…"

Kim always looks out for me by not letting people at work know my business, that's why I love her… "Ok, I'm in one of the doctor's office who's out today and I locked the door so that people can't see me through the blinds. What happened Girl?" "Darryl told me that he has HIV." I can tell that Kim was shocked, because there was a pause in her voice… "What?" "How did he find out that he had it?" "His job told him from a test he took at work, and the results came back showing he contracted HIV." "Is that lawful for a job to check on their employees' personal life by checking for that?" "He may have a lawsuit on his hand if they fired him."

"Well, Kim the way his job works is from what Darryl told me is they do physical check-ups every six month to see if they are capable handling long distance travel, and they offer STD testing by will, and if tested positive, they say it must be treated, if not treated, they could be fired." "Wow, I never heard something like that before, but in a good way, it's good to be tested." "So, you and Darryl broke up over that?" "No, it was because he blamed me for giving it to him." I can hear Kim cussing up a storm by now in rage and disbelief that this man would blame her Girlfriend… "I can't believe how stupid men can be these days!" Kim said. "I mean really?" "I should had known better than to get involved with a truck driver in the first place!" I said. "Then why did you Cheryl?" "I thought he was different from the rest." I said. "To be honest with you Cheryl, I thought he was different too." Kim said. "I should had been more careful." "Yeah Cheryl, I agree with you."

"Now you're going to have to get tested again, right?" "I mean you guys used protection, right?" (I didn't see this question coming and should had known it was coming…) "You hear me Cheryl?" (Now I'm embarrassed to admit the truth…) "Cheryl? Are you still there?" "I'm here, I was downing some water, what was the question?" "Don't play stupid Girl, I asked if you two used rubbers?" I took a big swallow… "No, we didn't." "Now, I know you have lost it!" "Cheryl, how could you not use protection knowing that this man drives trucks?" "I don't care what's going on between you and him and how good it was going. You still know better than that!"

"Anyway, enough putting you down, I'm here to help." "I know this Kim, but the only reason we didn't use protection is because he assured me that he was clean and couldn't have kids anymore because he was sterile." "Besides, my tubes are tied, so I wasn't worried." "Ok, so what are you going to do now?" "I don't know Kim." "I suggest that you get down to the clinic and get checked, just to make sure." "I guess you're right!" "But if it comes back positive, Darryl will have more to worry about than just his job once I get my hands on him." "I know that's right Cheryl!"

"Wait Kim I got an incoming call coming in hold on…" I looked at my phone to see who was calling… "It's Michael again Kim! He always calls at the wrong time!" "Cheryl take the call, I gotta go!" "This time hear him out so that you will know what's going on, ok!" Kim said. "Ok Girl, I will." "Bye!" Kim hung up. "Hello Michael, what is it that you want?" "You keep calling me over and over and I'm tired of you calling!" I shouted. But Michael replied with a soft tone to say… "Cheryl, please calm down. I won't be long with what I have to say."

"Say it Michael, so that I can move on!" "I've been to the doctor frequently lately, to find out that my health is failing rapidly." From anger I had, now turned into curiosity of what's going on… "Like what Michael?" "I contracted the HIV virus some time ago that grew into now full-blown AIDS." When I heard that from him, my mind drifted into one of those scenes for a "Lifetime" drama scene I watched on TV in the past. It's now happening to me, and I can't believe it! "You have AIDS Michael?" "When did you start noticing the symptoms…" As he was explaining it to me, my heart felt empathy for him, even in a dark moment of my time, I could have enough heart to reach out to someone else who's hurting.

"It started when I would stay ill from colds, flues, and fevers, with high temperatures that I couldn't shake off." "I've began to lose weight quicker than I would gain it." Michael said. "Then I would notice a breakout on my face, on my arms and chest for no reason like never before." "So, I would see the doctor, who later diagnosed me with pneumonia, that aggressed to full blown Aids." After hearing all of this, I forget whatever troubles both Michael and I had, for it was of the past, and I really wanted him to get better, but until I said... "Michael, I'm so sorry to hear this, but why are you telling me all this?" "Are you planning to die soon?" "It's not like you've been in Sabrina's life, so I'm sure she's not going to miss you." I said in spite that came out of nowhere... "No Cheryl!" "I don't expect to die anytime soon if I can help it." "But out of consideration, and the fact that you were my wife, I thought you should get checked just to be safe and to make sure you're ok."

After I heard what Michael suggested, I began to laugh in amazement that he would ever think of me now. "Now, Michael let's think for a moment..." "We've been divorced now for over three years; don't you think I would had done that by now?" "Especially what you did, and who you did it with?" "For your information, I had myself checked immediately after I left you." "So, don't worry about me, but yourself!" "I understand Cheryl how you feel, and maybe I had that coming, but at least have it checked again just to make sure that you are good." Michael said. "Thanks for sharing your concerns Michael, but I must tell you that you are a day late and years of nasty hidden secrets short!"

"You should have thought about all of that before you decided to destroy your families' life." "I'll talk to you later Michael, bye!!" I hang up the phone now feeling more troubled, because he wants me to be tested for a reason I cannot understand, but a minute later it suddenly hits me to the stomach that made me feel sick and light headed from all that he said.

I'm sitting down thinking how to put all of the pieces together, but couldn't come up with a solution or immediate answers why is all this happening to me! I'm just like many women who've been heartbroken from a marriage, who felt they've done the right thing to get married and have a family, but those dreams shattered by infidelity of the other spouse without regards who they may be hurting. I suddenly feel a breakdown coming from past and current blows in my life that I didn't deserve. I quickly get up from the couch to the kitchen, to see if I can find any alcohol to calm me down. I opened the refrigerator to find a full bottle of "Moscato" wine in the back hardly touched.

I take it out and open up for a glass to find, but then I said. "For what? I drink it as it is from the bottle!" So, I carry slowly the bottle back to the couch to try drinking my problems away until... "Lolol!" "You know what!" "I'm giving up on men altogether, because they all make me sick!!" "I might as well be by myself and I don't ever have to worry about anyone ever hurting me again!" "It's over! It's over!!!" I shouted so loud I can feel my chest vibrate after that shout. I mean I was done that night. Luckily, Sabrina didn't witness any of that, especially seeing her mother laid out on the couch with an empty bottle of wine left on the floor… Few days later, after being convinced to get tested talking with Kim, I had enough nerve to go forward with it.

My reason only was to prove to Darryl that I wasn't the one who gave him the HIV virus. So, the next day after leaving the job early to get tested, I walk in the clinic feeling numb and embarrassed having going through this at my age. So, I walked into a crowded little waiting room that looked dingy from the lighting and the floor had a slight odor from old carpet or mildew smell from past heavy rains that must had got in but dried. The walls were newly done from wallpaper that gave it a bright look of clean appearance. The crowd was many of people, young women with their kids, waiting to be seen. At one point, I felt like I was the oldest person in the room, until I saw the nurse, who appeared older looking than me at the counter taking information from patients; I felt slightly better, now that I've seen her. While waiting for my name to be called after I signed in, I get the feeling of discomfort of eyes looking at me, both men and women, I tried not to make eye contact for I was feeling embarrassed already for the purpose why am here in the first place.

But I could almost read their thoughts… "What she's doing here?" "What did she do?" "I wonder who she did it with?" Whatever they're thinking was, it's really none of their business. I know I'm not supposed to be here no more than them. But there was one woman who wouldn't give up staring at me for no reason, and I wanted to say something but I was already too tired to fight with anyone after all I've been through. What nerve does she have to be staring at me anyway? She looks to be out of shape, don't know how to dress, and her hair, her hair, whoever her hair stylist needs to be fired, lol! Let me stop! "Ms. Cheryl!" "You may come with me!" The nurse shouted. "Here I come!" I shouted. I say to myself… (It's about time, because another minute, I was ready to put a whooping on Ms. Younger version of Esther from Sanford and Son, lol.)

CHAPTER 11

Who's Fooling Who? – Craigslist Encounter Call

TWO MONTHS LATER NOW IN THEIR NEW HOME, BOTH Roderick and Sheila slept to a comfortable California King size bed, in their well-furnished home; cuddled together on a sunny Saturday morning, the sun shines through the double paned window, to reflect against the dark cherry wood floors, that illuminated the entire room. "Ding, ding, ding" … (sounds of alarm clock) Sheila rushes to hit the snooze button in disgust… "Ugh!

How did I forget to turn off the alarm last night?" Sheila rolls over facing Roderick as he is comatose snoring away in his sleep, she stares into his face trying to study his thoughts, but annoyed by his further snoring, she decides to pick at his big ears in hopes it would quiet his snoring… "What are you doing?" "If it ain't a booty call, then don't wake me." Roderick said with a grumpy voice. Sheila sits slightly up with her arm while her elbow rest on the bed looking at him to say with a soft voice… "No, it's not a booty call, but if you can put me back to sleep, maybe it will." Roderick's eyes open wide with excitement from hearing what Sheila just said to roll over to meet her face to face and said… "Well in that case, turn over and assume position, so I can rock that back to sleep."

"Uh, come again?" "You not going to get it that easy Rod, so try again." "Ok, let's do doggy I gotcha." "Boy you crazy, lol!" "For right now, settle for this kiss (smooch)" "Well, that's for start Sheila, lol!" They rolled back on their bed while staring up at the ceiling in a daze and a sigh of relief of their achievements… "Anyway Sheila, things are looking up for us, we worked hard to see this day." "You betcha sweety, we did." She said as she laid her head on Roderick's chest in deep thought, while he sat up against the head board day dreaming…

"You know what Rod, since we have an extra room not occupied, why not adopt a child, so that we can be a family." "Gee Sheila, I don't know." "I didn't think you would be up to having children after the last miscarriage." "I tell you what, Sheila I got an idea!" Sheila rose up with curiosity… "What Rod?" "Why don't we try again making our own?" "What do you mean by making our own Rod?" "I mean just that, we get busy in the bedroom and keep trying, you know?" Roderick said with excitement in his eyes. "You never know Sheila; it might work this time!" He said with a smile. Sheila looks at him with disappointment and irritation in her voice...

"Honey, why is it that every conversation we have it's about sex?" "That's because I'm horny!" Roderick said. "Well, see that's your problem right there; it's every time I try to have a serious conversation, you want to go there!" Sheila raised her voice. "And what's wrong with that?" "Ain't you my wife?" "Didn't that come with the marriage vows?" "I mean we ain't dating no more, so you should come through when I wanted!" "Now wait a minute Roderick, I'm not your home or some heffer on the street!" If I'm not in the mood, it ain't going down and that's that!!" "So, don't come at me about some marriage vows; I'm your wife, not a play toy." "If you don't like it, then find you a hoe on the streets or some blow up doll that will be at your every service!" Sheila said.

Roderick now frustrated and angry, he gets up from the bed to throw his arms down in anger, then looks at Sheila to say... "What's gotten into you lately Sheila!" "I mean before you would be begging me to get into the sheets before I can get in the door from work, but now, you act like I'm some stranger to you!" "Is there something I need to know about or what?" (Roderick stands back to now observe Sheila...) "Are you seeing someone else?" Roderick now asked with concerns and serious look. Sheila rolled her eyes at him to say... "Wow!" "You got some nerve to even accuse me of seeing someone else." "I should be the one asking you the same questions Mr. Pornstar!" Roderick paused a second in amazement, surprised what she just said. "Pornstar?" "What are you talking about Sheila?" "Where did that come from?"

"The last time you decided to look at men and women having sex on our computer!!" Roderick now stunned with a frozen look on his face… "That's right Roderick! You are busted!!" His first thoughts were (She must had found out I was on Craigslist…) "You wanted to start something Rod?" "Let's finish it!" Sheila shouted. "So, start explaining!" Roderick gives that innocence look, but cleverly tries to get information out of her of what she may know… "Ain't been looking at no porn Sheila!" "What are you getting at with this?" He asked. "I'm talking about the last time you gave me the computer while watching your father in the hospital, and you forgot to cover your tracks by not erasing or closing out the page you were in!" "Just imagine my embarrassment, here my own so-called faithful husband, gets caught looking at filth while I'm sitting in a public hospital room, for anyone to see that includes your father, imagine that!"

"So, don't try to lie your way out of this one Mr. Jackson, you are busted!" "I mean Roderick, am I not good enough for you?" "Ok baby you got me." "I was tripp'n and got drunk that night from all that has happened with Pops, so I got curious that's all." Roderick gets back on the bed where Sheila laid to say… "It wasn't nothing, I promise you." "You mean more to me than that crazy stuff." "So, my ba'ad fo-real." Sheila paused to process and think all that he had said for a minute, and to see how sincere he was… "Alright Rod!" "It's ok now!" "It's been awhile back since I discovered it and didn't really know what to think of it." "But you just need to keep it real with me, and not let things get out of hand." "You are right Sheila." Roderick said. "My concern though why is you looking at men having sex with other men?" Sheila asked. "Oh baby, I wasn't even tripp'n off them or paying attention to that." "I was more into looking at the women what they were doing, then it changed to that other junk." Roderick said convincingly.

After that conversation, Roderick sees an opportunity to change the subject... "Now about adoption, I'm all for it, so let me know when you want to do it, in the meantime, can a brother please still get some loving?" He said begging. Sheila paused a bit, then thought about his plea... "Alright Rod!" "Let's not ruin the morning about all this, so come get some of this loving that don't dry out..." "Thought you knew by now..." Roderick said. So, they both get back into the covers to kiss, touch, and grind each other until, Sheila suddenly jumps up by pushing him back off her... "Wait a minute!" "I think I feel something coming!" "What honey what?" "My period!" "So, we can't do nothing right now sorry!" "Awe Man!" Roderick gasped.

"But I'm not sure so let me go check it out." "If I'm not on my period, I'll make it up to you tonight, I promise." Sheila said assuredly, as she hurries up out of the bed to head toward the bathroom... "And if you still behave yourself, I'll let you hit some of this... (Sheila walked off smacking her butt) "I wish I could hit some of it now!" Roderick shouted. "Not yet! Got things to do, so get your mind right honey!" Sheila closed the bathroom door and locks it... "Why you locking the bathroom door for!" "Scared

I might come in!?" Roderick shouted. "Yes! You did it before!" Sheila shouted behind the lock door."

Now that the noise of a shower running behind lock doors of a bathroom where Sheila now takes her shower, Roderick leans back on the bed to hit his head against the backboard out of frustration to say to himself… (Hang it up, she ain't giving it up this morning! This pisses me off when she does that! Every time she promised to give me some, I get aroused for nothing but to disappointment when she doesn't come through.) "Man! I need a release and I'm tired of giving myself a helping hand when I got a wife!"

As he sat and pondered on what to do whether to begin his day to prepare to watch basketball "March Madness" college games or to give attention to his unfulfilled release for satisfaction… "Tell you what I'm going to do, look at some porn for a quick release!" "Thanks Sheila, for making my morning…that's messed up!" Roderick sneaks up out the bed and heads out the room to fix his problem, but before he does, he heads downstairs to the kitchen to get a cold gravity beer, then proceeded back upstairs to the guestroom to unload while Sheila is still in shower.

After 30 minutes later trying to get situated with the computer on porn websites… "Awe shoot, I hear footsteps! Sheila must be out of the shower and bathroom already!" Sheila walked out of the bedroom looking for Roderick… "Honey, where are you?" Roderick thinks in his mind (Great! Now she wants it) "I want you to tell me if this outfit would look right on me?" Roderick quickly to shuts down the computer, then rushed to the nearby hallway bathroom unnoticed… "Where you at Boo?" Sheila noticed he wasn't in the guest room to see a closed hallway bathroom door, so she knocks…

"Are you in their Rod?" She knocks again… "What do you think Sheila!" "Ain't nobody here in this house but you and me!" Roderick said sarcastically. "Ok, be a smart mouth about it, and see if you get lucky tonight!" "I'm about to finish dressing and then head out to the mall; Did you want to join me?" Roderick pretending to be on the toilet by flushing it so that Sheila can hear the sound of it… "No, you go ahead while I chill out to watch a couple of games and later go see Pops, to see how he is doing." "Alright Rod, suit yourself." Sheila walked away from the bathroom door to head back to the bedroom finish dressing. Roderick let out a sigh of relief…

"Man, that was a close call." Roderick slowly opened the door and heads to the bedroom where Sheila is finishing up before she gets ready to leave… "What's that you're wearing?" Sheila looks back at Roderick as she puts on her earrings before leaving "What did you say honey?" "I said what's that your wearing? You're planning to go out looking like that?" "Yes, I'm planning to leave like this…why you ask?" Sheila replied. "Don't you think you're showing too much cleavage?" Roderick said with humor in his voice. "Boy shut up, lol!" As Sheila grabs her purse, she gives Roderick a peck on the cheek to say… "I'll see you in a bit honey!" "Babe, you smell good!" Roderick said. Sheila looked back and smiled "Thanks honey!" "Oh yeah, pick me up a six pack before coming back home!" Before heading out the bedroom, Sheila stop abruptly to turn around to say… "Don't you think you need to slow down on those "Four Locos" or whatever you be drinking?"

"Well, first of all they ain't "Four Locos, it's gravity beers and you know it." Roderick replied. "Yeah, I know it alright, but I still feel that it's making you loco-crazy, lol!" Sheila said laughly. So, Sheila left after that. Feeling too relaxed from the beer he had earlier, he decided to go back to sleep. Two hours past, Roderick slowly woke up from a nap to head downstairs to the refrigerator to get another cold beer and a snack, takes a couple of sips wile tumbling through mail Sheila left behind on the kitchen counter… "Hmm, this is what I get for buying a new house, more bills, lol!" Roderick left the mail back on the counter while taking a bite of left-over meatloaf Sheila made last night until… (Ring, ring, ring) "Hello!" "Hey honey it's me!" "What are you doing?" "Sheila asked. "Just eating up your good meatloaf you made" (smacking while eating) "Lol, must be since it sounds like you're tearing it up!" "I give you that Sheila, you can cook!" "Anyway, what's up?" "Nothing, just called to see if you're still planning to see your Father if not, I will."

"That's cool, I've been feeling a little tired, but if I feel up to it, I will meet up with you later." Roderick said. "Alright, hope to see you than… Bye." Sheila said. Roderick puts his cellphone down on the counter while finishing up the rest of the meatloaf, the phone rings again… "What's up did you forget something?" Roderick asked, but no response until… "No, but was I supposed to?" Roderick stunned for a moment realizing it wasn't Sheila's voice, but a seductive luring voice of a woman. "Who's calling?"

"This is Trina calling for Roderick – Is that you?" "Yes, it is but do I know you?" "Well, again this is Trina, you responded to my ad on Craigslist some time ago." Roderick not able to recall what ad he responded to because it has been a while back, he decided to go along with the conversation just for the fun of it… "Oh yeah!" "How are you doing?" He asked.

"I'm fine, just thought to see if you're still interested?" "I'm sorry that it took so long to get back with you." "I had to go over-seas to deal with family issues, so I'm back." Trina said. "I tell you what, it has been a while since I've been on Craigslist and my mind is a little blank from all of this, so if you don't mind, please refresh my memory what your ad said and how you look." Roderick asked. "Not a problem, my ad says looking for a tall guy who likes oral." "I'm 5'8" athletic built, light skin, mixed with Black and Japanese Asian, long hair to my back, 145 Ibs, and well-shaped wearing red lace top and black tight shorts…" "Does that ring a bell now?" Trina asked. Roderick suddenly felt an erection from what she just described and her voice that captured him bondage to her call, had an idea of what she looks like, but not totally convinced that he remembers her… "Tell me what people say you look like?" "I don't know, but I've heard that I look like Chili from "TLC" or Nicki Minaj. Trina said. Suddenly, Roderick's memory kicked in after she said that, his heart began to race and his hands became sweaty from the excitement of her call… "Are you still there?" Trina asked. "Oh yeah! I'm here!!…"

"Oops, don't mean to get loud with that um, um, what did you say your name was?" "Trina, are you ok?" "Yes, of course, lol."

Roderick had to pick his face up from the floor, from the shock who he's talking to, a live fantasy. "You are beautiful, and I just love your voice that I can't stop talking to you lol." He flirted. "Thank you for the compliment." "So, are you still interested?" Trina asked. Roderick takes a big sip of his beer, to gather his thoughts… "Yeah, yeah for sure!" "But before we do, could you please describe yourself?" Trina asked. "Yeah, I'm 6'4, athletic built, with a baby face look alike Damian Wayans as I was told. Bald and beautiful and aim to please, lol!" Roderick said. "Oh really?" "It sounds like you are kinda cute." Trina said. So, what's it going to be?" "Are you available to meet me now?" Roderick smacked his forehead in disbelief that she would actually be that bold to ask… "Now? Meaning like right now?" Roderick asked. "Yes, like within the hour – will that be a problem for you?" Trina asked. Roderick hesitated to say… "No problem, let's meet" "Great!" "It won't take long unless you… (Roderick interrupts Trina to say…) "That won't be a problem, no need to explain." Roderick replied.

"Let's do this!" Roderick said. So, he gets all the information and place to meet up with her and time. "Got it Trina!" "I'll meet you at your spot in 30 minutes…bye!" Roderick said. "Good! And don't be late, or you just might miss out!" Trina said. The call ended. After hanging up with Trina, he begins to think… (What in the hell did I just do?) "I must be crazy; I can't believe I actually went through with this." "It's like something just took over my mind and thinking…" "Am I crazy?… "Maybe I do need to stop drinking like Sheila said, because it may be messing with my head." But soon after that reason to not go through with it, comes another thought… (But remember, Sheila has been tripping lately in the bedroom and haven't been fulfilling your needs in the bedroom, and you haven't had a good release in a while.) (Besides, it is not sex really but oral, and it's not like I'm paying for it or even cheating…) After being convinced with his thoughts, he says… "It's on and poppin!"

CHAPTER 12

Hidden Enemy – Big Sister Call

I FELT A MELTDOWN COMING TRYING TO COME ON me, due to all the stress that is happening to me all at once; Being a single parent who tries to do right, now dealing with resentment, anger, and hate from two bad relationships that left me scorned and bruised. I don't think I could love another man again after this! But after calming down a few days later, thanks to my girlfriend Kim, who gave me the guts and courage to go to the clinic to be tested again, I knew with confidence that I would test negative, and prove Darryl wrong. Just when I thought matters could not get worse, it did. The test results came back positive for HIV! The war is now on!!

While trying to stay focus to put the pieces of the puzzle together from all of this, I had to take a leave of absence from work, to keep from losing my mind. The attention now is to figure out who gave me the virus?... Darryl or Michael? But it wouldn't make any sense for Michael to do this because I was tested clean after I left him. So, it must be Darryl the truck driver, the ho driver, the liar he is! Several days later… The phone rings several times, but I didn't feel like picking up the phone to more bad news. (Ring, ring, ring) "Ugh! I give up!!"

"Hello!" "Cheryl! Where have you been?" "And why aren't you answering your phone?" At first, I couldn't make out who it was until… "Gina, is that you??" "Yeah girl! Yo big sista back in affect!" Now Gina and I grew up in separate homes because we have different fathers, but with same mother. We went to the same schools which made us close sisters. She was known as "BG" in high school and also in prison. When they heard that name "BG", people knew that she was one who took care of business both in the streets and prison, she was no one to play with. She was a bully to both the guys as well as the girls in high school, so it continued even into her adult hood, because she had so many connections that would come to her help anytime she needed is why people feared her.

Although she was looked to be feared and respected, she too had a weakness like anyone else. She experienced heart breaking relationships both with men and women, she realizes now that she can't trust nobody but herself. In prison, she stood for something different than the normal, she was a person at her word. What she said what she will do, she did it. She spent the last 10 years in prison from a botched robbery over drug money that found her guilty as charged. "So, Gina, when did you get out of prison? And when was you going to tell me?" "You don't pick up the phone! And I said to myself if she doesn't pick up this time, I'm going over there in person to kick her butt, lol!" "And don't think I haven't gotten word on you for I have!" Gina said.

Soon as I heard that, I suddenly became concerned about the STD test... "What do you mean by that Gina?" "What are you talking about?" "Since I couldn't get in contact with you, I had friends who knows your girl Kim, so I contacted Kim and had a long talk with her to find out you got a new squeeze in your life, and how busy you've been with this guy." Gina said. "Is it like that Cheryl? He must got it like that, where everyone else became last on your list."

Now I feel sicker from what I'm hearing from my big sister not knowing to be happy or sad. "So, where are you at now Gina?" "I'm at one of my girlfriend's house kicking it. But anyway Cheryl, the good news is that I've been trying to tell you is parole people decided to let me go early and cut my time in half, so they let me go home – Ain't that cool?" Gina said. "Yeah Gina. I said with a low tone voice. "What's wrong Cheryl? You don't sound too happy – What's up?" "Nothing's wrong Gina." "It's just I haven't been myself lately." "Like what are you talking about Cheryl?" "You supposed to be happy no matter what, now that you're sista is back in affect, you know that you can talk to me." Gina said. "I know Gina, and I appreciate it, but I've been under the weather lately, working a lot, while dealing with Sabrina now that I'm a single parent." Now Gina is one who can tell if someone is lying to her; it sounded good and probably convincing, especially dealing with my sister who knows me well, knows how to read between the lines as well as street smart, but to find out to my least expectation, it worked. "So, tell me what's going on with you and this new squeeze who stole your heart?" (That ain't all he stole) I said to myself. "So, come on girl! Quit playing and tell me what's going on with you and this new squeeze?" "I hear you guys kind of serious!" (Now why is she asking me all these same questions at a time like this I ask myself.) She must know something or Kim must had slipped and told her that I went to the Clinic. It's almost like she knew what's going on and was waiting for me to tell the truth.

"Nothing much more than what people do Gina." "It's just casual dating for now." "Besides, he spends a lot of time on the road as a truck driver, so it's not like we really have time for each other." "Ok, so when will I get to meet this guy?" Now I'm getting agitated with the repeated questions, hoping we can move on to something else. I'm really beginning to think Kim told her everything about this… "Why are you asking me Gina?" "I heard that you two make a good couple and I wanted to see for myself." Gina replied.

Before Gina could say anything else, I just folded with no longer pretending and had no more excuses of what I'm really feeling, so I burst into tears that I couldn't control… "What's wrong with you Cheryl?" "Why are you crying?" "Talk to me Cheryl!" I've managed to gain my composure for the moment while sitting down on my bed to explain what's really going on… "I contracted the HIV disease from Darryl!" I said while crying. "From who?" Gina asked. "From Darryl the new guy!" "You mean this new guy you've been seeing?" Gina asked. "How did you let this guy do this to you?" (Now Gina maybe street smart and seemed to have all the answers, but there are times she would ask some of the dumbest questions like this one.) "I didn't use protection because he assured me that he was clean and sterile; so, I took a chance not using protection knowing that I was clean too." "So, this fool lied to you so that he could get some and was dirty from the beginning; and you say that He's a truck driver that means he's been getting it from every trick on the streets!" Gina said. "How could you not pick that up still?" "I mean this fool been playing you, and I need to show him something because don't nobody play with my Sista for a fool!"

"But that's not all Gina, He's telling me that I'm the one that gave it to him!" "Oh, he dead now!!" Gina said. "Tell me where he lives, because I'm coming over there with some boys of mine, and we gonna to take care of that for ya! Gina said. "But before you do Gina, there's more to this story I must tell you." "Oh, get it out now, because I'm pissed off, and ready to do something about it!" Gina said. "Another piece to this puzzle is you remember Michael my ex, and how he did me too that destroyed our marriage?" "Yeah, I remember so what?" "Well, Michael called after the bomb dropped with Darryl, telling me he too has the HIV that now turned into full blown aids." Gina paused for a minute with no answer, sensing that she now confused at the situation… "Man Cheryl, I don't know what to think." "I was gone away from home to return to some serious drama – that's messed up!" "How are you taking all this?" "That's just it Gina, I can't take anymore drama like this." "I must try to keep it together for Sabrina's sake, for I am her only support she can depend on. Besides, I need to figure out what went wrong." "But Cheryl, didn't you say that you were clean with Michael?" "That's right Gina, I did say that." "The confusion to all of this is who's telling the truth? Michael? Or Darryl?"

"It's easy to blame Michael since he got caught with a man, but than it is also easy to blame Darryl since he's been involved with different women as a truck driver." "Michael however, seems to think it is him that gave me the HIV disease." "But why would Michael be thinking that?" Gina asked. "Because he feels strongly that he is the blame and wants me to get checked to be sure." "That was man of him to do that!" "He kept it real!" Gina said. "So, what are you going to do?" "My plan is to call Darryl over, so we can settle this problem once and for all… the truth!" I said. "Do you need anything from me?" "Like what Gina?" "Like come over there and jump'em!" "No Gina, but I tell you what you can do, pick up Sabrina and keep her for a couple of hours until I resolve this matter myself with Darryl." "It's time that I fight my own battles." "Alright then, if you say so." "If anything changes and you need help, let me know." "If you need a burner, I got you." (Confused at what she just said…I asked myself, what is a burner?) "Gina, what is a burner?" "Lol, sis you really are old school, it's a gun!" "I'm good Gina, at least for now, lol" "We'll take care that fool if you need me, just holla!" "Thanks Gina! I'll keep that in mind…"

CHAPTER 13

Who's fooling Who? – Seduction Hits

TWO HOURS PAST AFTER RODERICK MET UP WITH Trina, he returns home with no Sheila in sight. Feeling mixed emotions of guilt and indulgence, Roderick doesn't know where to begin putting the pieces of the puzzle back together as though nothing happened.

After getting settled that evening, he asked himself the question… "How can one person have that much control over another person?" "The question is was it worth it?" (Ring, ring, ring)

Roderick sitting on the couch in the living room staring at the television that's not on, steadily in deep thought not conscious of his surroundings… (Ring, ring, ring) Roderick snaps out of it to hear his cellphone going off… "Hello!… Hello…!" Caller pauses until… "Are you ok?" "Do you feel better now?" The soft voice of seduction said. "I hope you've enjoyed it as much as I did." Roderick looking puzzled, not knowing who the caller was… "Who is this?" "Was it that good that you forgot who you were with not long ago?" "Don't be a stranger now, it's Trina. She said with seduction in her voice. Roderick suddenly felt drawn to the voice that forever changed his life as if he was under a spell to say… "Yeah, I'm alright." He said but dazed. "So, tell me, what made you decide to answer my ad on Craigslist?"

Roderick finally gathers his composure to be attentive to the conversation… "I was curious for the most part until I found out in the last two hours the shock of my life that you are… (Roderick studders) "What Roderick?" Trina asked. "A man!" Roderick said. "Put it to you this way, don't feel too bad because many guys were fooled at first glance, and never knew until I told them that I was a tranny, and I'm not out to play games." Trina said. "Besides, I'm more a woman than man." "But still, you are a man and you fooled me to believe that you were a woman!" Roderick contested. "It wasn't me that fooled you Roderick, you fooled yourself." "I'm proud of who I am and I don't hide it." Trina said.

"But I met you in the women on women section of Craigslist, where I thought I got lucky a woman made exception to her ad!" "So, tell me, you really don't remember where you met me other than my ad itself?" "Well shame on you than, because if you had looked carefully, you would had seen "TW" next to "WW" Trina said. "Ok, I got it!" I hit the wrong sight by a mistake." Roderick said. "Was it really a mistake Roderick?" "Think about it." "What happened tonight wasn't a mistake now was it?" "When you finally met me, your eyes and body didn't say it was a mistake, because when my touches and my red voluptuous lips touched all over you, it wasn't any longer a mistake in your mind then, so don't say it's a mistake now." Trina said.

Roderick now stunned at her comeback and comments, he had to run to the fridge, to grab a quick gravity beer to gulp down fast to drown his guilts and shame... "What are you doing Roderick?" "Did I mess you up again? Lol!" "Real funny Trina not laughing." "Don't be mad now, at least you got the best of two worlds, lol!" "Ok Roderick, let me stop playing, but seriously, you can't take it back so what are you going to do now?" Roderick now feeling the quick buzz and now has drowned his feelings aside, he begins to say... "The thing that gets me the most about you are how good you look, and better looking than most women I've seen, but really a man." "I really didn't know what I was getting myself into, and my intentions was to be meeting a woman."

"So, what are you saying Roderick? Are you disappointed?" "When I was with you, the woman you were looking for you found." "Don't be confused, remember how this fine light skin was all over you, and how you told me I smelled like sweet apricot perfume, how you touched my smooth skin, and how the lips did wonders while my long hair tickled your stomach and chest, and how you loved it and said repeatedly "I want more!" and I gave it to you." "Remember that?" Trina argued. "What about how I had you were screaming for more, remember that?" Trina said with seduction.

Roderick's head spinning from the amazement how Trina talked and had him hostage at her voice, he became a prisoner of her seduction all over again… "Wow! You are good!" Roderick said. "I do my best." Trina said with confidence. "I mean you almost had me convinced, but still having trouble shaking off you're still a man." "Don't worry Roderick, I'm confident that in matter of time, you won't even remember any thoughts of me being a man, or past tensed was a man." "I'm more a woman you ever dreamed or imagined, promise you that!" "I'm very assured who I am, and my experience with other men has proven, that they not only loved it, they became possessive and I had to put a stop to it." "I don't like guys who think they can treat me like a hoe or prostitute!" "I like the same thing that any woman would want in a man that is respect!" "So, don't think Roderick that you can pull one over me, because I can assure you, I know all the games and I will beat you every time."

"I posted my ad with the intentions of meeting a nice guy who wanted to get to know me other than what my ad said for Oral, for I like Oral as in communication more than what's typical of what we often define." "What are you talking about Trina, I thought your ad meant sex!" "No, it's more than that; I'm saying the right man who stimulates my mind orally can get what he wants, so far that is you Roderick!" Roderick begins to think to himself."

(Damn, I can't remember what the hell I said that night, but it must had been good!) "Just so you know Roderick, you were one of the few that had a chance to taste more of me, because I'm attracted to you." Trina said.

After smacking himself on his forehead, Roderick says to himself (I'm screwed!) "Are you still there?" Trina asked. "Yeah, I'm here!" "Just can't get over how I missed all that, and how far I got without noticing it!" "Well, don't worry." "If you let me be a woman to you, I promise I'll be less a man I ever was." Trina said. A call came in on Roderick's phone between his conversation with Trina... "Hey Trina hold on for a second, I have a call coming in..." He clicks over... "Hello!" "Hey Son!" "This is your Father, am I interrupting you? Or is this a good time to talk?" Roderick immediately sits up right from his chair feeling sudden condemnation... "Oh, hey Dad!" "No, you're not pops, but hold on I had another call waiting... Roderick clicks back over to Trina where she was on hold... "Hey, Trina my pops is on the other line and I..." "Hello?" "Hmm, she must had hung up."

He clicks back to his father... "So, what's going on Pops?" Roderick panted. "Just doing good son, are you sure that I'm not interrupting anything?" "No, I was talking with a friend while moving some stuff around the room (I hope Pops could forgive me for lying...) He said to himself. "Well, I called to let you know I'm doing better thanks to your wife Sheila at my bedside." "Is she still there? No, she left not too long ago, but I wanted to be the first to tell you that the doctors are relieving me next week and I'm good to go." "That's good news Pops!" But there was a short pause… "Pops, are you still there?" "I'm here, I just wished that you were here to see how well I'm doing, lol" "Pops, I look forward to seeing you before they release you, I promise." "Thank you, Son, that's all I really wanted to hear." Roderick had a moment sigh of relief. "I see you soon Pops; I love you." "I love you too son!" "I will be there next week to pick you up!" "That sounds good son, I look forward!" "Goodnight pops!" "Goodnight son!" "Oh, before I forget, Sheila didn't look too happy; why don't you give her a call before she makes it home." "Good idea Pops!" "I will!"

Roderick begins to think to himself… (Something isn't right with Sheila, my father feels somethings wrong even in his time of sickness, he can see Sheila isn't herself.) (It can't be what I did with Trina, because she has no clue what happened…) (I'll figure it out before Sheila can say anything…) "It's 11:00pm, where is Sheila!" "She left the hospital almost two hours ago, after Pops, told me when she left." Roderick looks through his text messages to find that Sheila text him over an hour ago to say "Honey, I tried calling you and you did not answer, anyway I'm at the store picking up a few things and will be home late, I love you. Bye" Roderick now trying to figure out how did he miss her message earlier, but gets ready for her to come home anytime now… (Sounds of the door opening…) That must be Sheila!" Roderick runs down the stairs to greet her to see her tired and out of it… "Hey honey, I got your message, sorry I didn't call you back, I was talking with Pops…"

Not responding to what Roderick said, Sheila walks slowly into the kitchen to put the things she bought down with no eye contact or excitement to see him, but pauses a moment, then looks at Roderick with her bedroom eyes, soft chocolate skin that had no feelings for him there. Roderick reached out to kiss her but she moved back as she continued to stare at him as though confused with whatever she's feeling… "Baby what's wrong? Are you ok?" Roderick asked. "I'm ok why you ask?" "You don't seem your normal self." "I'm good, just tired." "I'm going to bed, please put these up for me." "Ok honey, I love you!" Sheila didn't respond to what he just said. Roderick says to himself feeling guilty… (I wondered if she found out?) (That can't be because she wouldn't have known what happened earlier.) (One thing I do know, ain't no loving going on tonight.)

Four weeks went by… (Ring, ring, ring…) "Hello!" "Hey son it's me your Father." "What's going on Pops?" "I know it's been a while since I've promised to see the house you and Sheila bought, so I thought this may be a good time since I'm in the area visiting members from the church (If Pops shows up tonight, it would be perfect for Sheila since the house is fixed up for showing after she had bought so many new things to her liking… "No problem Pops!" "About what time were you thinking?" "About 8:30 son and I won't stay long since it was unexpected." "Cool, we will see you soon!"

Just as soon as Roderick hangs up the phone, an incoming text from his cell phone came that read "Didn't I blow your mind?" Soon Roderick realized it was Trina to say to himself… (This whatever got me twisted.) So, Roderick decided to call her to say… (Answering machine picks up…) "Oh, she doesn't want to answer now." "Hello Trina, I'm leaving this message since you didn't pick up, to say I'm not interested, and whatever happened between us was a mistake because I was drunk and didn't know what I was doing. So, I'm sorry to say please lose my number, it was a pretended fling, it won't happen again, bye!"

After hanging up, Roderick begins to question himself... "I thought she moved on since I haven't heard back from almost a month now!" "Why text me?" "I was hoping that she lost my number or found someone else." "And how in the hell did I not pay close attention what section of Craigslist I was in!" "How did I miss the fact Trina is a transvestite?" "Does that mean I'm gay?" "No, because I felt she was a woman and not a man." "If I wanted to be with a man, then I would be with one, but because I don't like men doesn't make me gay now." He justified.

"I can't tell no one of this, and no one need to know, and I will take this to the grave as a deep secret, even Sheila won't know." "Since everyone sees Trina as a woman, then I leave it as that, she's a woman for all that concerns." After series of questioning himself, rubbing his face out of frustration, he hears the door slam from the garage... "It's Sheila!" Roderick fixed himself up to greet Sheila from a long day... "Hey baby!" Seeing that her mood hasn't changed for a while which is cold, Roderick tempts to grab her hand in a moment of compassion until... "Roderick stop, I'm not in the mood!" "Hold up baby, I'm just trying to welcome you home can a man do that for ya!" He asked. Sheila continued her dried cold mood until Roderick said... "Pops will be here in 30 minutes to finally see the house!"

Suddenly, life came into Sheila and aware of Roderick in front of her... "Really?" "When did you find out about this?" Roderick looking surprised as what was once dead now came back to life, Sheila... He called some time ago saying he was going to be in the area and wanted to see the house as promised." "Oh, I must hurry and fix up the house and freshen up baby!" Sheila said. She now ran up the stairs with sudden energy to get prepared for her Father-in-law visit, Roderick looks over the counter to see "KFC" for dinner... "I barely get any loving, so now the cooking for me is gone and she just going to leave a brotha out of luck to be with a 3-piece meal when she knows I eat more than that!" "Now irritated, he slams the meal down, while complaining still, he heads up the stairs in anger to confront Sheila to discover she's already in the shower, preparing to meet his father, he gathered his composure to say... "I'll let her slide on this one..."

30 minutes later... (Doorbell rings...) "Sheila Pops here!" He yelled from downstairs. "Ok honey, I will be down in a minute, and make sure you don't smell like alcohol!" Sheila yelled. Roderick opens the front door to greet his Father... "Hey Pops you finally made it!" Roderick's father overwhelmed with joy greets his son who stands about same height 6' 4" with same caramel colored as his son, but skin and face reflection of older and wiser from colored snow white gray beard and bushy hair, wearing his favorite brown Kingston hat matching his overcoat... "Come in Pastor Palmer Jackson!" "Thank you, son Mr. Roderick Jackson! Lol" Roderick embraced and hugged his father as they stood in the foyer of his home.

As they were discussing amongst each other comes Sheila coming down the stairs; Roderick and his father looked up to notice how gorgeous and beautiful Sheila appeared. Roderick began to think to himself as he admired Sheila… (Man, God really blessed me with such beautiful cocoa sweet chocolate in that nice dress looking like a bride all over again, I must be a fool to even risk losing Sheila). Roderick's father turned his attention to Sheila with a big hug… "Thank you so much for being by my side during my stay at the hospital." "Your welcome father, I was glad to be there for you and to be by your side, that's what family do." Sheila said. "My daughter you look fantastic, and I'm proud to have you as family and my son's wife." Roderick was in agreement as he put his hand around Sheila's shoulder. Sheila noticed his gesture by smiling up at him and to grab his hand to hold to say… "I'm glad to be part of this family and for you to be my father-in-law."

Roderick's father attempted to get settled as he admired the house, he notices a picture of big in size the sitting room of both Sheila and Roderick's wedding picture… "My-my, that was a beautiful day when I first married you two." "Yes, it was father, and I thank you for doing that." Sheila said. "The home looks beautiful; I thank God how he has blessed you both with your own home." "Have a seat Pops!" Roderick sits next to his father on the love seat while Sheila sits across. "So, Sheila, how is you and Roderick doing?" "He's not giving you any trouble, is he?" "If so, let me know, I will take care of him, lol!" "No, he's no trouble father but I will sure let you know when he gets out of hand, lol." "Very funny you two very funny, lol!" Roderick said.

As Roderick continued to joke and talk a lot, in close proximate, his father suddenly gets a whiff stench smell coming from Roderick... "Roderick what's that smell on you?" "What smell Pops?" Roderick's father continued to sniff his son's shirt to ask... "Have you been drinking son?" Both Sheila and Roderick looked with surprise on their face of what their father just said. Roderick responds to say... "Yes Pops, I have." "It was just a glass of wine to relax from a busy day, lol" "It smells like you had a whole bottle of it, be careful of that!" "Most certainly Pops, I will and apologize for that." To help quickly change the subject, Roderick asked... "What do you think of the house?" After asking the question, he glanced across the table to look at Sheila's expression after that revelation from his Father, he noticed in her eyes a volcano ready to erupt from the embarrassment. "It's nice son, I love it." "Let's take a tour of the whole house really quick before you leave Pops, I'm sure that Sheila is anxious to show you around." "Great! Let's do that." "Yes Father, I will while Roderick goes freshen up quickly right Rod!" "Yes baby, I will be right back!" Roderick quickly runs up the stairs to get rid of smell of his breath, Sheila continues the tour... "I have a house warming gift for you and Roderick wait just a minute I'll go to the car to get." "Ok Father I'll wait for you."

As Sheila watched her father-in-law go the car to retrieve a gift, Sheila fought inside mixed emotions to whether yelled out at Roderick for embarrassing her or to relax and wait for right moment to confront him. Soon after that thought comes her father-in-law with beautiful adorned baby blue combination with goldish color wrapping with baby blue big bow to match... "Here you go but it's a little heavy let me sit here on this foyer table." "Oh, father you didn't have to go through all this trouble for us." Sheila was surprised how beautiful the gift was wrapped, it almost reminded her of the great day of her marriage to Roderick… "It's beautiful father." Roderick running down the stairs hearing the commotion to say with a smile… "Hey what's going on with all the noise down here, lol!" "Look Roderick, your father gave us a house warming gift!" "Cool Pops! Thanks." "Well you two, opening it, lol" They unwrapped the heavy seemed box to discover… "Aww, how nice!" Table setting for 12, complete dish ware with gold trims that so happened to match the gold frame of their wedding picture. "How perfect Father! I will put this in our dining room." "Thanks Pops! You've made our day." "You both are welcome." "Now that I have you two here together, allow me to share some things before I head back out.

They all went to the family room to sit on the couch while this time Roderick sits with Sheila as their father sat across from them… "Allow me to ask this question…" Both Sheila and Roderick looked at each other with a blank look not knowing what to expect… "What's on your mind Pops?" "How are you two getting along?" After hearing that, Roderick began to think to himself (I wonder if he knows I've been doing something behind Sheila's back?) (Maybe he's about to give me a lecture on drinking?) Sheila sat puzzled thinking… (Why is he asking this question?) "We're doing great as you can see Pops! Right Sheila?" Roderick knew he gambled asking that knowing he hasn't had any loving from Sheila almost 3 weeks… "Yes honey, of course!"

"That's great son to know." "Because I know how hard it's been on you two getting over the miscarriage, so I wanted to comfort you and assure you both it's never too late to have children, even if you have to consider adoption." Both Sheila and Roderick sat back in their couch with sigh of relief until… "Another thing I wish to ask, have you two been praying and studying together?"

Before Sheila could answer that question, Roderick quickly responded to say… "Well Pops, we've been busy and admittedly slacked in that department." "With our conflicting schedules with my job and her home business, you being sick, and our transition into a new home has limited our time do that." "As soon as the dust settles, we will get back on track." Roderick justified. Sheila nodded her head in agreement. "Well, don't let it get away from you, for a family that prays together, stays together…" Sheila interrupted to ask… "Reverend Jackson, would you care for something to eat or drink?" "No dear, I'm fine." "Now like I was saying…" As the Reverend talked, both Sheila and Roderick hoped this conversation would end soon for they felt enough guilt as he continued to talk…

"Now let me finish by telling you this…" Both Sheila and Roderick sat pretending to be intuitive of what was said but felt more unedge saying to themselves… (Wish he would get up and leave soon) 30 minutes later… "Well, I think I said enough and must be going!" Both Sheila and Roderick jumped up with excitement to say… "Thanks for coming over and the gift!" Sheila said. "Yeah Pops, we appreciate everything and stopping by." "We'll be in service on a regular basis in a couple of weeks after the "March

Madness" is over." Roderick said, but Sheila quickly corrects him to say… "Uhm, what Roderick really meant was we will be in service real soon." She looked at Roderick with piercing eyes in disgust. "Great! I will be looking forward seeing you both!" They all hugged each other and wished their Father off as he left. As Roderick closed the door and locks it. Sheila looks at him in disbelief… "Roderick why would you say something as stupid to your father the Reverend about going to church after the basketball season is over?" "Stop trippin, I know my father." "He always trying to get me to do something I'm not ready for by scaring me to come to church or his health failing so that I can take over his church!" "He's just looking out for you and wants to see his only son do right." As Sheila was talking, Roderick began to notice her cleavage and how the dress she wore revealed the fine shape of her behind, Roderick's attention focused more how soon can he get in the bed with her than what she was saying and feeling… "Well that's cool and all, but right now what we should be doing is relieving each other after a long day." Sheila looking puzzled not knowing what he meant… "What are you talking about Rod?" "You know what I'm talking about! Getting some like now!" Roderick giving her the funny looks with great anticipation…

"How could you be thinking about that, when your Father was just talking about us getting right." Sheila said. "The only right I'm thinking is right now heading right upstairs, right in our bed, and get this sex thing right once and for all!" Tension and irritation surfaced from Sheila to say… "That's all you ever think about is sex!" "You never want to hear me out or attend to my feelings, we don't even talk like we used to like friends and lovers, you don't even make me feel like a woman anymore, you don't answer my phone calls and you don't explain or say sorry or even why you've been distance from me." "You haven't been the same Roderick in a month and don't know why or what I've done to deserve this." "You act like sex is the only thing important to you in the world!"

"Is that what you think about while at work or when I'm not around?" "That's right! Every time you diss me or flake out on me!" "I think about it in the morning, at noon, and all night long!" "Because it's like this, if you don't want to meet my needs, maybe someone else will!" Both Roderick and Sheila were shocked what was said. Roderick caught himself and knew he said it out of frustration realizing he said it out of anger. But at the same time, arrogance kicked in to say… "The problem with you Sheila is you don't want to fulfill your wifely duties." "As long as I could remember, the bible says I'm the head and the wife supposed to submit to my needs, if that's a problem let me know!" Anger surges from Sheila to say… "Don't get smart with me Roderick! The bible also say husband to love their wife which is something you stopped doing, so don't play me for a fool and don't even try bringing the bible in this conversation!!" "I'm your wife, not an object or your sex toy!" "When I'm ready to have sex, is when I feel I'm being loved not when it's forced!" "So, you tell me who's been holding back? Is it me or really you?" Sheila walked off after saying that to head up the stairs for bed until Roderick says… "Screw you Sheila!!"

Sheila continued up the stairs to shout back… "Screw yourself Rod! That seems what you do best!… (Door slammed.) Roderick says to himself… (This is crazy!) (I give this woman everything a woman could ask for and this is the thanks I get!) Roderick in his thoughts as he secured the whole house for the night. He heads upstairs to the bedroom in hopes Sheila would change her mind to be in better mood for some loving, but to discover Sheila already undressed and tucked in the bed done for the night. "It's like that Sheila?" No response from Sheila. "Well screw you Sheila!" "Leave me alone Rod, and screw you too." She muttered. Roderick changed clothes into his pajamas, then grabbed his cellphone to leave the room… "Where are you going Rod?" Sheila asked as she raised up her head to see what Roderick was doing. "Where do you think? Away from you!" Roderick said. "Bye!" She said. Roderick slammed the bedroom door as he left. "Stop slamming my door Rod!" She shouted.

After Roderick left the room, he hears Sheila's footsteps toward the door thinking she was getting ready to open it, instead he hears clicking as she locks the doors to their bedroom… "Fine! Lock the doors!!" He shouted. After that, Roderick decided to chill in the guest bedroom for the night, but before he does, he heads back downstairs to the fridge to get two cold gravity beers, to take immediate gulp of the first one then heads back upstairs to settle down.

He takes another gulp of his beer to feel the drink going down his throat strong into his stomach, to feel the numb he was looking for and at total relaxation forgetting all that happened earlier between him and Sheila. He sat up on the bed, grabs the TV remote to turn on the television to flip to the sports news. He looked at his phone and noticed he had several missed calls from an unknown caller and had a text that read "Why do people pick-up a magazine and don't read it?" "Why buy a new pair of shoes and don't wear it?" The text messages read. "That's weird!" "Who would send me that crazy text?" As he continued finishing his first can a beer while watching the sports news, out of curiosity, he gets up quietly to lookout the room to see the bedroom if anything may had changed, it didn't. Back in the guestroom, Roderick locked the door behind him to prevent Sheila from walking in. He sat back down on the bed to grab his computer he finally bought for himself, to see if he had any emails.

As he was scrolling, he had a thought that just made him stop scrolling... "This thing still haunts me as to where did I really meet her in...Why don't I go back in that listing, the ad to find out if I actually made a mistake her being a woman or not by meeting Trina months ago!"

He scrolls down and notices other trannies in "TW" but no Trina. "Maybe she took her web page off..." He looks harder again with no luck and was ready to get out of the section until... "There it is! Under the older classifieds of this site!" As Roderick begins to study Trina's page, he says to himself... (Man! I can't get over how good she really looks!" He noticed she added newer photos of herself and kept the old ones, Roderick noticed the very photo that changed his world, he found Trina in provocative positions and poses in tight black screw me shorts showing off her feminist of her legs and thighs, in her robust breast covered in red laced topping, and her red voluptuous lips, her Asian eyes dressed well from the make-up and long hair to the side as she laid on her stomach showing off her backside, the more he studied that picture, the more he became horny with lustful thoughts and fantasies that polluted his mind.

Now on his last beer, his mind filled with all kinds of erotic thoughts and all morals has went out the door. He is now wasted; all barriers or cognitive thinking has weakened. "If I give it one more chance, would it mess my thinking up?" "Naw, because I'm only dealing with the woman side of her and not the man." "I just want some oral anyway, so it wouldn't hurt. It's just a fling and it will be over just like that." Somehow after all he had planned, a thought of caution, perception of danger came across his mind to say... "Don't do it, for it might hurt you or worse..." (Man I need to quit thinking crazy again and leave it alone!)

So, Roderick quickly gets out of the site, closes out his computer and powers down. Just as soon as he shuts down his computer, comes an incoming text... "Still waiting for your answer!" Looking puzzled, Roderick says "Who in the hell is this texting me?" Just as he finished reading the text the phone rings from his cellphone... "Hello!" "Hey, it's me again." After hearing that, the voice sounding soft and sweet, he asked... "Who is me?" "Trina, who else would you expect?" Roderick first had a blank look on his face, but soon remembered... "Oh Trina? What's going on?" "Nothing much." "You've probably didn't recognize my number, I changed it soon after you and I got together." "Are you saying that you never got my last message?" Roderick soon realized that she never got his last message that read "lose my number not interested" "No, I never got your message, but so much has happened since then, I didn't want you to think I wasn't interested." Trina said.

"So, when will you answer my question?" "What question?" "The one I text earlier." "Oh, that was you?" "Ok, but I still don't understand the questions you were asking so fill me in." Roderick said. "The question I asked why do people pick up and magazine and don't read it? And why do people buy shoes and don't wear them? Maybe it's because people are not satisfied and haven't found what they're looking, not knowing what they really want." Trina said. "Why respond to my ad, and don't follow through it?" Trina said. "Didn't I already pass first base with you? What more do you want?" Trina asked. Roderick, as he continues to listen to Trina, he says to himself… (Man, I never had anyone talk so much good game like that before) "I need for you to make a home run with me because I just might make you strike out." Trina said seductively. "Are you scared of me?"

Roderick finishes his last can of beer with one last gulp to say… "Girl you crazy!" "What does it look like a tall 6'4" guy like me be scared of a little woman like you." "Maybe you're scared that I might steal your heart in ecstasy and don't want to leave again." Trina said. "I got what I wanted and even more, so I'm good, and besides you are, are… (Roderick studders to finish his statement). "What Roderick? A man?" "Like I told you before and showed you, I was more woman that night to you than ever a man." "I'm probably more a woman to you than any other woman you have experienced, because I know what you like and I give it to you."

"I am one surgery away after many previous surgeries and hormone changes to be fully complete woman, so stop your worrying." Trina said. "But Trina look, the fact still remains that the thing that you have sacked in your panties is not in common what I want, it wouldn't work." Roderick justified. "What I said on your last phone number you had was this fling was all a mistake and it shouldn't have gotten as far as it did." "I'm going to chill out on this one, you hear me Trina?" "I'm not interested!" The line paused; Trina ignored everything Roderick just said by asking… "Did you receive my recent text with photo?" "What text? What photo?" "The one I just sent." "Check your phone." Roderick checks and downloads the picture that was sent… "Oh hell! No, you didn't!" "You got to be kidding me!" Roderick said from excitement. "What do you think Roderick?" "Does it look anything like a man to you?"

The picture she sent was of a seductive lingerie worn by Trina. A see-through blue lace short dress that showed all the feminist features of a woman; her curvaceous body the fantasy a man would want. "Wow! That is off the chain!" "How do you do it?" Roderick gasped. "You still didn't answer my question Roderick." "What, what was the question?" "Do you like it?" Trina asked. "Hell, yea I like it!" Roderick's beers now sunken in and taken a toll from the 12 percent volume of each beer can, his motor skills and speech now impaired fully drunk…

"Are you sleepy Roderick, I know it's 2am in the morning?" "No, I'm just trying to get over how good you look." Roderick now fully aroused at her picture; he now asks… "What can you do for me?" "What do you mean by that?" "I mean what can you do to satisfy me now?" "Satisfy you like how?" She asked. "Anything just do it." "Now we're getting somewhere, but how can I do that, if I'm not there?" Trina asked. "Just say something good and nasty to me!" "Aren't we straight to the point; but remember, I'm still a lady so don't think you can talk to me any kind of way, lol" Trina said. Trina now suspects something is wrong with Roderick… "Have you been drinking?" "Why you ask?" "Because you sound drunk." "No, I'm not drunk but relaxed." He defended. "Well, you definitely do sound and act like it." "Well, I had a beer or two." "It sounds like you had more than two beers, lol!" "Yeah, well you wouldn't be laughing if you knew how good I am in the bedroom after a couple of drinks, I would send you into ecstasy forgetting all about your troubles." Roderick said.

"Ooh, such big words require a big come back!" "I tell you what Roderick, I gave you something to think about the last time, now I'm going to give you something to remember that will make you want to come back for more." "What I say to you now, you won't be able to escape it, so don't say I didn't warn you!" "Ok, ok just do it Trina." What Roderick didn't know that he just sold his soul to the Devil… Trina began to talk dirty enough to Roderick that it made him explode in his pants so bad that he dropped his cell phone on the floor that accidently hung up on Trina during the climax of their conversation. Once after that, he regained himself and said (That girl got skills I've never heard and can talk game better than me as though she was here with me).

After several attempts to clean himself up from the beers he drank, suddenly he passes out on the floor from all the excitement and the toll of the drinks. The sound of a door slam wakes Roderick up immediately and the brightness of the sun's reflection from the window on his face, Roderick takes his arm to block the brightness of the sun in attempt to get up from the floor he slept all last night, to inquire the noise he just heard outside the guestroom. He looks around the room to find anything unusual for he doesn't remember all that happened last night. What was noticeable was he left on the bedroom light and tv all night as he slept.

He now reached for his phone to see it was nowhere around or insight. He panicked a little in search for it. Checked the bed and under the pillow but not there, checked the computer and noticed that he properly shut it down (Thank God I shut the computer down...) He continues to look all around the room for his phone, but to find two empty beer cans on the floor, so he quickly picks them up to dispose of it in trash can. As he proceeded to the door to investigate on the noise, he discovered his phone in the corner on floor near the tv. He looked at the time to see... "Man, its 10:34am on a Sunday morning!" He proceeds to check his phone for messages and discovered he had 4 missed calls: 1 from Sheila and 3 from Trina. But out of the 3 missed calls from Trina came a text that read... "I must had rocked the poor boy off to sleep." "Hmm, got jokes." He said.

Once he cleared the room from his junk last night, he then proceeded out the guest room to the bedroom to see Sheila was nowhere in sight, but a message on the bed that read: "Went to church, sorry for last night and I wanted to give you some, but you decided to leave the room and I said forget it. You know I love you and I want you and will be there for you honey, just promise you will be there for me. Again, I love you." Roderick now feeling guilt and shame now says to himself… "Now she was ready for me! How am I supposed to know that?" But he reads further in the note… "I also left you breakfast in the oven when you decide to wake up. Love and kisses." Roderick now relieved, but at the same time feeling guilty, he suddenly hears his Father's voice say… "Son, as you know, we reap what we sow…" While Roderick doesn't remember where that came from, thoughts now bombards his brain… (I need to stop all this before somebody gets hurt!)

CHAPTER 14

Hidden Enemy –
The Confrontation

LATER THAT NIGHT I CALLED DARRYL AND ASK HIM to come over so we can sort things out, he agreed without questioning. I personally wanted to confront him to get to the truth, so we can move on. Hours later, I hear the doorbell ring, but before I answer, I wanted to make sure my thoughts were together without my emotions getting in the way what needed to be said. I downed any wine left in refrigerator, and fixed myself presentable for this occasion… "Hello Darryl! Come in!" When I looked and observed him, I see that Darryl came dressed to impress, wearing blue jeans that hugged his thighs the way I like, and a nice polo shirt light green with matching hat and tennis shoes, wearing my favorite cologne "Dolce Gabbana" probably in hopes to throw me off… "How are you doing Cheryl?" He asked. "I'm fine." I said with firm voice.

In my mind, I say to myself (Pleas make it quick, so I can kiss this relationship good-bye!) Darryl's demeanor was not the same as it used to be, it was different and cold; he looked and observed my home as though it was his first time being here, or play private investigator seeking clues how he can close his case… "So, Cheryl, where have you been?" "It's been a longtime since I've heard from you." He said callously. He continued to walk around the living room, looking at the furniture to see if anything changed, and looked toward the kitchen to see if anyone was there to say… "I thought you might have a new boyfriend or something because you…" "How dare you come over into my house talking to me any kind of way!!" "You know where I've been!" I shouted.

My emotions went from 0 to 38, because now I'm livid, 38 hot in anger! "The question is why you lied to me about what you been doing!!" I shouted. "What do you mean by that?" He asked. "You can continue to play games Darryl; you know that you gave me this virus!!" He looked stunned and astonished at my reaction to say… "You're crazy!" He said. "I thought you had me here so that you can explain how I contracted the HIV from you." "You know perfectly well that I've been celibate until I met you!"

Darryl paused a moment to say… "Oh, I see now!" "Because I drive trucks from city to city, I'm a player who sleeps with every woman from city to city, right?" Now I know this relationship is over after that accusation. Suddenly I can hear that old song from Gladys Knight "Neither one of us wants to say goodbye" "Goodbye Darryl." I muttered. "What did you say Cheryl?" "I said goodbye, it's over between us!

I started to cry. "Get out for good, I never want to see you again!" Darryl tried to embrace me, but I pushed him away because he saw how hurt I was… "Please, don't touch me, I want you out now!" I opened the door for him to leave, he looked at me with puppy eyes, and walked out.

Two days later after leaving Darryl, I couldn't return to work just yet, because I was trying to adjust that I'm now single again. Just to think I once thought to have escaped the likely hood of having the virus to be proven negative of the test, here I have someone trying to accuse me that I gave it to him when I know I'm clean. I never thought Darryl could lie to me until now.

So, to avoid hearing from Darryl, I turned off my phone and stayed in silence to gather my broken heart back together. I now realize my greatest support in my life is my sister Gina, and my best friend and co-worker Kim. As far as I'm concerned, men have let me down again! One day after getting my head together, I've returned home from a long day at work with groceries in hand trying to unlock the front door with my keys, the door opens without my key to find out… "Ahh!!" I screamed. "What are you doing here in my house without permission and how did you get inside!!" I yelled. "Remember, you gave me a key." Darryl said softly. "You wouldn't return my calls so I figured you would be here around this time."

I put the groceries down on the couch without having to walk any further to protect myself... "What is it that you want Darryl?" "Give me my keys back now!" Darryl looks at the keys in his hands and looks at me then puts them on the coffee table in my living room. I quickly grabbed them off the coffee table in case he tried anything suspiciously. "Anyway, I came over to apologize for what I said and..." "Darryl, it's too late to apologize, it's over like I said." "Ok, ok but at least hear me out – won't take long. I looked at him to see the sincerity in his eyes... "Hurry up and say what you going to say Darryl." "I've been telling you the truth from the beginning about being clean and celibate, over two years until I met you."

"Just put yourself in my shoes, I work for a company that pays good and happens to be one of the few companies that requires physical check-ups of all matters including STD for their liability sake reasons to obtain employment." "It puts my job in jeopardy if tested positive in risk spreading to other people because of the line of business." "Do you obviously think I would be stupid enough to have a one-night stand to not only jeopardize my career, but also this relationship?" I lose everything that I worked for including you."

I think he's getting his point across with me because from one time being angry, now turned into inquisitive wanting to hear more, I suddenly felt my guards coming down and something telling me he's telling the truth... Darryl seeing the atmosphere of hostility changed to acceptance, he took the moment and chance to grab my hand and look deeply into my eyes to say… "Why of all things would I pass up a beautiful woman, who became my heart and what we have going on." He said softly.

"Two thing I realized that are more important to me is the job and you." "I've never told you this, but when we first met, my mind was made up to be with you for a long time." "What do you mean by that Darryl?" While Darryl continued to look deeply into my eyes, he says… "I love you and I'm in love with you." Once Darryl said that, I felt something strange come over me that made me surprised what came out of my mouth without hesitation… "I love you too Darryl."

As soon as I said that, the feeling of resentment now became warm and quivery all over my body. I knew than I was vulnerable to whatever next Darryl might say. "You see, you say that you haven't been with anyone, and I haven't been with anyone, and we're both claiming that we were clean before getting together than what is it?" "Could the report be wrong from my job and be a mistake? If not, then what?" After he said that suddenly I got scared of the unknown and said… "I don't know Darryl and now I'm really scared! I cried out. The security I once missed came to my rescue once again, he embraced me in his strong arms, placed his hands and fingers through my hair with much tender loving and care, and kissed my forehead to say… "Don't cry baby, we will figure this out together." "You don't have to worry about me going anywhere, I'm right here for you." "You're my woman and I'm your man!" What woman don't want to hear those true sentiments coming from a man, I miss hearing that from Darryl. "I got to go now, but before I do, remember this one thing…" "What's that Darryl?" "I love you." When we kissed it was nothing like anything before, it took my breath away, it was connection unbelievable; this kiss stole my heart, it was electric, I just can't explain it any better, it was magical that made me forget about all my troubles…

"I'll call you tomorrow to see how you doing and to see if you still want us to be together." I said to myself after he made that comment… (Is he kidding or what? After that kiss, of course I want to be together silly!) "Ok honey." After he left, my heart felt more for him to the point I cannot live without him. He kept it real with me and that is what I like in a man… Keep it real! Now I must still deal with the matter, who has this virus, and who really gave it to Darryl, this I must know. Once Darryl left, I went to my bedroom trying to figure out this situation and how he may had contracted the virus, whether Darryl's claim is true, or his exam is incorrect. I know it wasn't me that gave him the virus because I checked out immediately after I found out what Michael was doing, and my medical report said I'm clean.

So, Michael couldn't have given me the virus, for me to spread to Darryl. What I decided to do to help Darryl's assurance in me, I went back through my saved paperwork of my test results to show him the next time he shows up. But before I can dig any deeper, at first, she startled me because I was engrossed in thought searching for documents, but gain composure to welcome my little princess… (noises of footsteps coming closer to my bedroom door…)

"Mommy." I turned back to look at those pretty eyes in need for attention… "Yes baby, what is it?" "Come in!" Sabrina slowly opens the door to say… "I'm hungry and can't find anything to eat." "Baby, if you look in the refrigerator, you'll find tuna sandwiches in the clear container already mad along with chips on the counter." "But I don't want that mommy, I want pizza that's in the freezer." "Ok honey, but mommy is busy right now, so you'll have to settle for the sandwiches until I'm finished."

Sabrina walks out with her arms folded with disappointment in her face with her lip poked out. After seeing that, I was reminded how I did the same thing with my mother, not getting what I wanted. Hmm, lol…that's kinda cute seeing your child do the same thing you did. Once Sabrina left the room, I returned to my research looking for dates and time when it all transpired getting tested. I finally came across my divorce papers that was final over two years ago, then I came across my old medical records, test results showing negative and the time and day needed to show Darryl the next time he come over.

So unfortunately, it doesn't answer the question how did Darryl get it. So, I began to say to myself after finding my paperwork, out of love for Darryl, I will get tested again just to be certain it wasn't me. The next day I get tested at the clinic, the results are now positive I have HIV and wondered how this could happen when my first results were negative, so I asked the nurse was my first results a mistake. "Cheryl, the testing process that determines STD results are never tampered nor do they lie." "All test results done at this facility often come back 99.9% accurate whether negative or positive." The nurse said.

"What I don't understand is my test results were negative at first, but now positive. How can this happen?" "Have you been sexually active since your last divorce?" The nurse asked. "No, I haven't… (Ok, I lied. Didn't tell the truth) Before I was able to explain any further, the nurse tells me… "Test results are dependent on the time of inquiry. For example, you may had been very well tested immediately after suspicion for results to show negative, but after while it becomes positive after certain amount of time." "You were tested a day after your suspicion and most people would not have done that…" "Thank you for your time…" I said. After leaving the clinic, it became obvious who really gave me the virus… Michael! Now I'm mixed with different emotions from bitterness to now anger again.

Old wounds seemed to creep back while hatred seemed to have dominance over my feelings. At first, I felt the world coming down on me again, but this time from shame and embarrassment not believing Darryl by blaming him giving it to me. At this point, I wanted to kill myself or runaway, but I couldn't because of two people in my life love me and needed me… Darryl and Sabrina. If it wasn't Darryl pressing the issue about this, I probably be facing Aids like Michael is now without knowing it…

CHAPTER 15

Who's fooling Who? – High School Reunion

4 MONTHS LATER... "SHEILA YOU READY YET?" Roderick asked. "Almost, just about finished baby." Sheila looking over her black tight dress with gold glitter trimming coming diagonal hugging her athletic body, turns to the side to see all her curves looking to see if her stomach in and butt out in the right place... (Hmm, don't I look good) Sheila continues looking in the mirror to see if her makeup and hair is right... Roderick standing behind and grabs her by the waste line as she's fixing her lip gloss to say... "Baby, you know you look good!" He kisses her face

as she continues to fix herself. "Thank you honey, now move…"
She uses her hips to push him back. "I'm putting on my earrings
so I'll be ready soon." "Rod, don't forget to take with us my 2004
yearbook to the reunion!" Roderick picks up the yearbook and
thumbs through the pages to find Sheila's picture… "You know
honey, still look the same 10 years later…" "Really Rod, like how?"
"The same skinny cocoa puffs conceited hard to get woman, lol!"
"Shut up Rod, lol" "Let's get going babe, I don't want us to be late!"
Roderick said. "Stop your rushing we'll be alright." Sheila said.

"No, that's not true Sheila because you're always late for everything and you how I get about being on time." "No, your problem
is that you like to be too early like the time we were at the airport
3 hours early before our scheduled flight. And we're sitting around
in an empty section, no flight attendance to take our boarding
pass or nothing, looking like we lost, while people walked by, lol."
"No, that's not true because there was another time we were at the
airport and almost missed the flight because you didn't want to
run through the airport worrying if your wig was going to fall off
while trying to catch our last-minute flight, lol." "Wait a minute
Rod, you are not playing fair, lol." "And what's wrong with my
wigs?" "Oh, nothing wrong with it, except when we go there in
the bedroom it falls off every time, lolol!" "You stupid Rod! You
got jokes, lol" "Ok girl, we got to get up out of here, so let's go."

Now driving off in the car… "It's amazing that we both met
each other at the same high school, and now married attending
our high school reunion." Sheila said. Roderick listens while driving to say… "Uhm correction, your class reunion; I graduated in

2003, a year before you." "Oh yeah that's right!" Sheila said. "But who ever thought of gold and black colors for the reunion when the colors for the school was blue and white." "Watch and see if someone shows up with the right colors blue and white, lol!" Sheila asked. "Yeah, like who knows it might be your old boyfriend that shows up in them loud colors, lol!" Roderick said. "Whoa, sounds like someone is hate'n." Sheila said. "Hate'n? You got me messed up, hate'n on what?" Roderick asked. "It's been 11 years since I graduated, so why should I hate." "I don't know Rod!" "But since you brought it up, let me see who I can remember…Oh yeah! My best friend Shemika, and the guy I can remember you hate'n on was Trent." Roderick looked over at her as he was driving to notice that Sheila's eyes lit up as she thought of Trent. "Wow! That didn't take long to remember now did it?" Roderick asked. "Don't be jealous Rod, for it was a high school crush years ago."

"But I do remember how fine he was, like real light skinned cute guy with dimples with gorgeous eyes that every girl adored." Sheila said. "Oh, spare me the details Sheila." "And he was a cute light skin sexy guy…" "Ok, Sheila there you go again with the light skin dudes… Sorry I couldn't be any lighter for your taste." "Next time remind me to go lighter like Michael Jackson did; Rest in Peace homey!" "That's not funny Rod!" "If you really must know, Michael Jackson was really my boyfriend!" "Yup, and everyone else boyfriend!" "The truth is no player really could hate on Michael, we simply tried to be like him, lol" "Whatever Rod, lol"

"Well anyway, you didn't tell me much about this crush of yours before we got married, so you might as well tell me now and confess up!" Roderick said. "Oh, you mean Trent?" Sheila responded innocently. "I think his full name was Trent Williams, who once blew me a kiss to get my attention so that he could date me." "What stop that from happening?" Roderick asked. "Who ever said we didn't date?" Sheila asked. "Ok, my baad" Roderick replied. Sheila rolled her eyes in amusement to continue… "So, after we dated a couple of times, there came this stranger getting in the way name Roderick, lol" "Oh, so you saying I messed that up for you? My baad still, lol." "Hey don't be surprised if he shows up, ok honey!" "Gee, I don't know whether to run and hide or say good, maybe you two have a lot to catchup on and reunite." "Shut up Rod, lol" "Don't miss the turn to the entrance of the hotel."

Now at the Marriott hotel where they show up for the class reunion, the hotel is full to capacity, combined with both guests and visitors pictured like for a main attraction or event of the night. "Do you recognize anyone yet?" Roderick asked. "No honey, not yet." The parking lot appeared to be full as Roderick searched for a parking, Sheila roamed the crowed as they were slowly driving by to see if anyone she recognized. Finally, Roderick got lucky to find a parking spot. "Wow, it's a beautiful warm night baby!" "Yes, it is honey!" "This place is packed like in the club; I feel like I'm back in my single days looking for the ladies! Lol." "Shut up Rod!" "Keep it up, I just might let you have that moment if my boyfriend Trent shows up, lol." "Wow, I'm so, so scared!" Sheila hits Roderick on his back to say… "Get inside this hotel before I do something to you!" "Yes Ma'am, I behave boss!" Roderick said sarcastically.

"Do you recognize anyone yet?" Roderick asked. "No, I don't – still looking. Sheila roamed the crowded lobby while Roderick admired the many beautiful women passing him by... "Wait a minute! I think I see someone I know... That looks like Shemika, I think... Sheila drew closer to whom she thought to be her high school friend until... "Yup! That is Shemika... "Shemika!!" Sheila shouted. Shemika turned around and waved at Sheila... "Sheila?? Is that you?? Ahhh!" They both greeted and hugged liked they were from the two girls from the movie "Color Purple" "Girl look at you! Haven't changed a bit!" Shemika said. "Girl, what are you talking about, you haven't changed much yourself!" "Oh, stop playing." "I've gained 20 pounds since high school, while you look like you haven't gained yourself, except thicker in the butt, lol." Shemika said. "Well blame it on my active life and my squat exercises I do." Sheila said.

While Roderick stands in the background continuing to admire the women from abroad, Sheila finally brings him into the conversation... "Roderick! This is Shemika my old classmate and friend... Roderick looked down at Shemika's physical features that made him think lust thoughts... (Man! She is a fine caramel looking babe, but on the heavy side, got some nice breasts hanging out with that cleavage calling my name, but her long braids covering partially her breast is blocking my full view...) "Roderick!" Sheila yelled. "Pay attention Rod, the woman has her hand out." "Boy! I need a ladder to shake your hand, lol." Shemika said. Both Roderick and Shemika greeted each other while looking for a table. "Say, why don't we all sit together at a table, I'm by myself tonight." Shemika suggested. "Sure girl, that's fine with me if it's ok with Roderick." "It's cool with me besides, it's your reunion… I'm just a tag along." Roderick replied.

Sheila notices an empty table and hurried to get the table so the three could settle down… "I'm about to head to the bar for a drink, do you want anything Sheila?" "Sure, get me a martini…" "Did you want a drink Shemika? My treat." Roderick asked. "Yes please, I'll have the same as Sheila. Thank you!" "Roderick now leaves to get drinks, while the girls get reacquainted… "So, tell me girl, who's here that we can remember?" Shemika asked. "I got a yearbook we can go through, to see if we can recognize anyone while thumbing through the pages…"

They've searched through different pictures and remembered some old class mates from different sections, but didn't see if any were present until they looked harder to see how many people, they recognized present at the reunion have gained weight and shocked at the changes of some who were very athletic in their youth. It wasn't long that Shemika ran across a familiar face… "Look Sheila!" "You remember Trent your old flame?" "Yeah girl, of course I do!" "But he wasn't my flame, he was a crush." "Well let me tell you something that you may not know…" Sheila leans over toward Shemika with curiosity. "What's that?" "Trent is gay!" Shemika said. Sheila had a surprised look on her face to say… "What?" "For real?" "You're lying Shemika!" "Not Trent the track star!" Sheila said. "I couldn't believe it either Sheila, until it was confirmed with some other people that know him." "He was handsome and cute, I can't imagine how he looks now, maybe even more cute." "It is what it is Sheila."

While Roderick is at the bar scene, he waits for the bartender to get his attention to order his drinks… "Excuse me! I know that you're busy but can I quickly get two martini's and one Hennessy with coke!" Roderick asked. "Comin right up Sir!" The bartender replied. As Roderick waits for his drinks, he observes the bar and scenery intently around him… "Man! There is no one here that I can remember from this school." "Although I'm a year behind them, I would think to see someone that I know." But the only thing Roderick did notice is beautiful women sitting around engaging in conversations.

As the women would pass by Roderick, he made sure he gave eye contact with flirtatious expressions, letting them know he liked them. But to his surprise, they would flirt and look back at him with a wink… "Shoot! Only if I was single now, I would have all kinds of play!" "I got to be careful, mess around getting these women numbers, I would be in a world of trouble, lol." But there was one woman that caught his eyes that left him breathless. Sitting across the bar is this attractive woman wearing a tight gold glitter expensive looking dress, that hugged her whole body that left little imagination to the eyes. With long hair to her back, bold seductive demeanor while streaks of hair covered slightly over her right eyes with a curvy body that stood out as she sat on the bar stool slightly showing her sexy legs. Light skinned complexion with red bold lips, make up made perfect as though she was getting ready for a model audition.

Just as soon as Roderick would make eye contact with her, the bartender distracts him to say… "Sir, sir your drinks! It took a moment for Roderick to come out of what looked to be a spell, paralyzed from his eyes staring down this woman from total submission of his lustful desires… "Oh, oh yeah! Thank you!" Roderick said. He attempted to hold all three glasses at once, but realized it wasn't going to work without spilling one, so he took two of the girl's drinks and decided to hold back his to pick up later. He returned back to the table where the girls were to deliver their drinks… "Here you go Ladies!" "Thank you honey!" "I guess I'll leave you two again while I go get my drink now!" Sheila didn't say anything more but ignored what he just said because she was so engulfed in the conversations both Shemika and her was having while tumbling still through the yearbook. Roderick already felt extinct or invisible, so he left to return to the bar to retrieve his drink.

Upon returning, he noticed more and more people gathered where he first ordered his drinks, so he decided to go on the other side of bar to get the same bartender's attention… "Excuse me bartender!" "I'm back to pick up my other drink!" "One moment Sir!" While waiting, Roderick continued to roam the crowd, admiring the women far from him and distant. Then he turns back to the bar to have a seat and notices to his left a woman sitting two stools away from him, the same woman he admired earlier. He dared his pride and ego, to see if he still had the swag to see if he could get her attention and strike conversation… "Hey! How's it going?" The woman gave no eye contact, but continued to be entertained with her drink, while slowly spinning her straw, with callous response to say… "Fine."

Roderick felt the cold response and tempted to redeem himself from the cold blow, to continue with the attempt to gain attention… "You here by yourself?" Still, no eye contact from the woman, but now notices her getting irritated in his quest to conversate to say "It looks like it." Roderick, and his ego, didn't allow him to give up, but continued trying to break the ice… "Do I know you from somewhere? You look familiar!" Roderick saw that he wasn't getting anywhere until she looked at him and responded with another callous remark… "Really?"

Roderick now feels humiliated, but tries one last time to redeem himself to ask… "Hey, can I fill that drink with another glass?" The woman looked at him one more time to say… "No thanks!" "I can do that myself." Finally, feeling bruised, Roderick backs off after the many rejections he received. The bartender noticed his failed attempts but saved him to say… "Here you go Sir! I gave you another drink since the other one was old and watered down, but before you go, may I see your ID once again!" "Sure!" Roderick shows the bartender his ID and retrieved his drink. The bartender says… "Mr. Roderick Jackson, thank you!" As soon as the woman on the left sitting next to him heard his name, her attention was drawn to him.

The woman removes her hair that was slightly covered over her right eye, and now looks inquisitively at Roderick's face and said… "Roderick?" "Yes, that's me." She studied him more by looking at his face and body height to say… "You don't remember me or know who you looking at do you?" Roderick appeared puzzled and assumed it maybe an old classmate flirting with him and says… "Yes, I do remember!" "I'm looking at the finest, sexiest, and most attractive woman in this place… Any questions?" He said with a smile. After that compliment, the woman seemed less amused at his remark, but boldly leaned over toward him with a straight look to say… "It's me, Trina!"

Roderick, now in a state of disbelief, stood back in shock and embarrassment knowing that he just got over having a fling with a transvestite to now look at Trina, who looks more of a woman she ever would be. "Trina?" "But, but you…" "Shhh!" She said. "What are you doing here and why haven't you answered any of my calls?" Trina asked. "It's my wife's school reunion, I stopped talking to you because I made a mistake as I told you many times before, to focus on my marriage and I moved on as I thought you did." "She's here with me tonight." "But until now!" Trina replied with a smirk on her face. "What do you mean by that Trina?" "What's that supposed to mean?" "You know what I mean, so don't play stupid now!" "Your wife would applaud you on your acting skills on faithfulness you displayed minutes ago." Trina said with a smile.

Roderick feels a little guilt, but quickly changes the tune by drinking down his Hennessey and coke, to ask quickly the bartender to give him second round of Hennessy straight without coke to say… "Fine Trina, have it your way!" "I always do Roderick; thought you knew by now!" "Anyway, what brings you here?" Roderick asked. "Oh, I'm here on business." Trina said. "Business?" "What business?" "You here with a client or something?" Roderick asked. "Now, I know Mr. Faithful is not getting jealous!" "But, if you must know, it has nothing to do with that." "What you should be more worried about is why you still here talking with me instead of your wife!"

Roderick quickly orders another refill on his drink straight Hennessey without coke again and says… "You got all the sense in the world huh Trina? We ain't done yet!" "Done Roderick?" "You've made that clear months ago that we were done, so what changed now?" Roderick looks around to make sure Sheila or her girlfriend didn't see him chatting with another woman to say… "Just meet me in the lobby in 10 minutes." "Don't want to be seen talking to…" "Another woman Roderick?" Trina interrupted. "I'll give you that, since you do look good tonight, don't be late!" Roderick said. "Look who's barking orders tonight, lol!" Trina said. "So, when will I have the honors of meeting your wife Mr. Faithful?" Roderick quickly looks at Trina with a serious look, then downs his last drink to say… "Not tonight, not ever!" "See you in a few…"

Roderick walks off. Trina now thinks to herself and say… (He thinks he's getting away dissing me all this time, and thinks he's running things, hmm, he got another thing coming to him, he's been warned! … As Roderick rushed back to join both his wife Sheila and her classmate Shemika, he notices that he wasn't missed too much to say… "Hey what's going on honey?" Sheila looked up at him to say "You ok?" "Yeah, I'm ok why you ask?" "Thought we lost you, because you've been gone a long time." "We missed you for a minute, trying to order a refill on the Martini, but you weren't here, so I took care of it already." "I'm good, the bar was a little more crowded the second time when I tried to retrieve my drink." Sheila was convinced what he said, then turned back her attention to Shemika, reminiscing on old times.

15 minutes went by, few more old classmates joined the table where Sheila and Roderick were sitting along with Shemika, sharing old times. Roderick notices the time past to meet Trina and says… "Sheila! I'm going to run to the restroom, be right back!" But Sheila paid him no attention as she continued her conversations with old friends. Roderick says to himself… (Man, she is all into her own thing and really, I could had stayed home, she really didn't need me to be here.) Now seeing it was a goodtime to escape from Sheila's company, he left to proceed to the lobby searching for Trina to tell her it's not safe to be seen in public ever again until… "Looking for me?" Trina grabbed Roderick's hand then pulled him closer, to embraced him while others looked with approval. Roderick suddenly felt trapped in his mind from Trina's cruel seduction and hold, he gets a whiff of her perfume that didn't help matters, her beauty, and sex appeal left him vulnerable under her control. "What's wrong Roderick?" "Are you nervous?" "You keep looking around like you are hiding from the law or your wife!" "I'm fine Trina." "Then stop being so nervous and scared like somebody is going to catch you." "I'm not worried about anything!" He said with arrogance. "Oh really? Let's see…"

By surprise, Trina grabbed his face, to give him a big kiss, while Roderick jumped back to say… "What are you doing? Trying to get me killed or something?" "Lolol, poor Mr. Faithful, can't you see?" Roderick now looking puzzled. "Listen, why don't we play this off like nothing never happened." Roderick pleaded. "Oh, it's too late for all that Mr. Roderick, for you can't turn back the hands of time. What was done is done." "What do you mean by that Trina?" "Oh, you know what I mean, don't play stupid Mr. Roderick." "You took the goods and think you can cancel everything all of a sudden." "It doesn't work that way with me. The last person who tried that died, thinking he could get away with it." Roderick stepped back and wondered to himself and asked… "You killed him?" "No, silly!" He killed himself, because I wouldn't take him back after I left him from cheating. He said I would die for you if you don't come back, I said well, that's your problem, I have nothing to do with that, we're done here. So, he shot himself in the head." "You got a hold on people like that Trina?" "Not really, but if you do me wrong, it somehow comes back on you, lol."

"Enough of that, back to you…" Roderick said. "Look, it was obvious that I was drunk that night and wasn't thinking what I was doing, or getting myself into." Roderick justified. "You didn't seem to be that drunk when you did it the way you did with me that night." "I'll never believe that!" "Look, stop your worrying!" "I'm not going anywhere, for I will be here for you." Trina said. "Ok, this what I'll do, I'll pay you off so that you can leave me alone, will that take care of everything?" Trina looked, smiled and laugh to say… "My dear, you don't have enough money in the world to pay me off or change my mind. Do I look like I'm broke or something, lol" "Besides, stop your worrying for now, as you can see, people here don't disapprove our company.

Your wife obviously isn't thinking about you, so we might as well catch up on some things…Trina took full advantage of his weakness by grabbing his hand to caress it and pulled his waist into hers, then put her arm around his neck and look deeply into his eyes as her breast pressed against his chest and the perfume smell now leaving him hostage of her seduction to now putting a big kiss of his life that he couldn't fight off any longer, than Trina slowly released him as she slowly released the touch of her lips off his lips to see what his response would be… "You got me twisted and can't seem to get out of it." Roderick said. "I thought you knew, Mr. Roderick!" "You now under my spell which was the whole purpose!" "Spell? Maybe for now but… (Trina steals one bigger kiss long enough where Roderick was fully under Trina's submission, he squeezed Trina's butt as they are kissing, but quickly stood back in a trance… "I know I shouldn't have done that. Roderick said. "You didn't… I did." Trina said, as she caressed his face and then walked off. Roderick now feels defeated.

CHAPTER 16

Hidden Enemy – The Breakup

AFTER IT WAS CONFIRMED THAT I HAD HIV contracted from Michael, I called Kim for moral support, but by coincident as I was dialing her number, comes an incoming call… "Hello!" "Cheryl, It's me Michael." "I know who this is!" "What is it that you want, and why you keep blowing up my phone calling me so much!" "Hey, hey no need for all that right now." Michael said. "Don't tell me how to speak on my phone, seeing that you are the reason for my attitude!" "But while I have you on the phone, let me ask you something… How long has it been since you decided to stick your head in a man? How long Michael? And how many times did you do this while you were with me? Can't hear you! Speak up!" Silence was for a moment on the end of the line... "I guess you can't talk right now, must be busy with something down your throat...I hate you Michael!! I shouted. "You've ruined my life and the life of another person who had nothing to do with this by your selfish acts!" "If I had a gun, I shoot you for what you did to me!" "What did I do to deserve such punishment from you!" "If you hated me so much, you could had just told me!" "Instead, you wanted the best of two worlds!" "Speak up Michael!!" "I can't hear you!!" I shouted. After that, I noticed still the phone was silent for a moment until... "Shut up already!" "Just shut up already!" Michael shouted.

"Now you listen to me, I didn't mean for all this to happen." "Didn't have intentions to hurt you!" "Last, I am not gay!" "It was a time of curiosity that just happened until you caught me." "What in the hell does that mean Michael?" "You sound like a hype, or jay on drugs!" "It only takes one action to be gay!" "If that's what you wanted, I could had least been given a chance to give it to you. It's your life!" "It's your opinion Cheryl, not a fact." "You're right Michael, it is my opinion, and the fact is I have HIV, due to your actions!" "Look, if you're going to keep yelling, we can just end this conversation." I began to hang up the phone until he says... "I'm sorry again how it concluded to this, but you must now deal with the consequences like I am." "Consequences Michael??" "Consequences come when people make decisions to do good or bad and willing to take whatever comes to them." "In my case, I didn't have that choice, nor did my boyfriend, that's right! My boyfriend, who now has it, thanks to you!!" "Neither I, or my boyfriend had the chance or luxury to choose!" "It was chosen for us by default!!"

"So, once again thank you for ruining our lives and Sabrina's life who grows up without a father! Bye!!" "Wait Cheryl wait!" I hung up! Two days later I called Darryl to say… "Hey baby it's me Cheryl." "By chance can you come over this evening to see me?" "Sure, baby what's on your mind?" Darryl asked. "We need to talk about something in person that will help me to clear up what's on my mind." "Ok, we can do that, but can I get a clue what's it about?" "I will tell you when you get here, but for now I got Kim calling on the other line, I'll see you then baby, I love you." "Ok, I love you too. See you later." "Hello!" "Hey girl, long time no hear." Kim said. "Girl what are you talking about, it has only been two days, lol." "So, what's up with you Cheryl?" "Girl it never fails, just when you're on the phone with someone else, the phone blows up with another call, but when you're not on the phone, nobody thinks of you, lol." I said. "Yeah, that happens to me too, but at least you're laughing about it which is good." Kim said. "So, what's going on Cheryl?"

"Well, I finally got to the bottom how I contracted STD, and who gave it to me." "Wait a minute, wait a minute Cheryl!" I can tell this was a shock to her because I just now realized I didn't tell her that I actually went back to the clinic to be tested again during that two days off… "I thought you said your first test results were negative?" "Yeah true it was, but after talking with the nurse at the clinic, STD doesn't always appear right away or immediate. It can take weeks or even months for it to be detected. That is why they say if you are sexually active, it is good to be tested, so that you can know who the person that gave it to you." "So, Darryl gave it to you trying to lie about you gave it to him, right?" Kim asked. "No, it wasn't Darryl." "Who Cheryl?" "It was Michael." "Wow Cheryl!" "I'm so sorry to hear this." "It makes me sick to the stomach that Michael hid this from you all this time." "Why can't men ever be real!" I can hear the anger in Kim's voice after hearing the news… "It's tough enough that we got to deal with their lies and cheating with other women, now you got to worry if men are bi-sexual in these times." "I got more respect for a person who come right out and say they're gay, then a person who hides it and pretend to be heterosexual!" Kim argued.

"That's not all Kim, even married, you got to wonder if you need to wear protection in a marriage, in fear of your spouse is cheating…" I said. "I here you Cheryl, but protection doesn't always guarantee it will work, especially in Michael's case; Which reminds me to ask, do you know if Michael was wearing protection when you caught him?" "No Girl I don't know, for I was already traumatized from the whole situation." "I didn't tell you before, Michael called to tell me that he has full blown aids and could die soon." "Wow Cheryl!" "Things just don't get any better do it?" "Does Darryl know about this?" "No, not yet but will tell him tonight when he comes over and to tell him I'm breaking up with him after the news I got from the clinic." "You mean to tell me you're still going through with it after he accepted you back?" "To leave him even though it wasn't your fault?" "Yup! I am." "I had enough drama in my life, dealing with relationships in my life."

"Besides, I now have to live with the guilt, giving Darryl the virus, I never knew I had." "But Cheryl, you both now have it, and it's treatable." "Don't you think he might want to work it out?" "Maybe so Kim, but I don't." "After all that has happened, it's too much to deal with and having the reminder every day that I ruined his life – No Thank You!" I said. "Well, let me know how it all worked out." "Good luck Girl!" Kim said. "Thanks, talk to you later…"

Several hours now passed, anticipating Darryl's arrival. Trying to gather the facts and my thoughts before he gets here… (Doorbell rings) At first, I would be excited to see Darryl, like a child would when a parent gives them their favorite Ice cream cone, but today it's different… "Hey Darryl! Come in." This time, Darryl is wearing casual beige shorts with pearly white sneakers with a white "V-shirt" to match. Looking sexy and smelling good, but at all times I would be thrilled, not today. I give him a quick peck on his cheek and welcomed him in… "Did you want something to drink Darryl?" "No, but I brought something special that you may like." He pulls out this big clear bottle… "What's that Darryl?" "It's a Donald Trump brand that came out in 2005 called "Trump Vodka" Darryl said. "It looks expensive Darryl; I hope it didn't cost too much." "I don't put a price on my love for you Cheryl." Boy, there he goes with the words that make me melt into his hands…

After we had a couple of drinks, while sitting on the couch, I began to feel mellow and relaxed to share what was on my mind, while Darryl sits next to me with his arm over my shoulder as we drank… I looked up at his bold sexy eyes, and began with a soft

voice to say… "Hey, I called you over here to tell you something."
"I'm sure that you got the drinks in hope I would tell you something good, but it's not." Darryl's facial looks changed from anticipating good news to now puzzled not sure where this is going…
"What's on your mind?" He asked. "I couldn't get over the fact of
you blaming me for giving you HIV, so I did some research." "Ok!"
He said. "Remember when I told you I found my ex-husband
cheating, and I divorced him for that?" "Yes I remember, what's
the point?" "The point is I never told you that he was cheating on
me with a man not another woman." "He contracted HIV, which
is now full-blown aids." "So, that means I contracted the virus
from my Ex, and in return gave it to you, not knowing that I had
it." After giving Darryl the devastating news, from once mellowed
out mood from Darryl now came the anger, I was prepared for…
"You mean all this time, I was thinking you were cheating on me,
to find out you had this disease all this time, and decided to give
it to me??" "Now wait a minute Darryl!" "Just please hear me
out!" "Had I known that I had this disease, I've wouldn't have got
involved with you or anyone else." I was assured at first, when the
test results I had before showed negative, but this time the second
testing showed I'm positive." "I never would had checked it again
if it wasn't for you blaming me for your virus, and my Ex pushing me to get tested again, I've still be in the dark blaming you."
Darryl sitting back on the couch rubbing his head in disbelief, I
went further to say… "Darryl, I know what you're thinking, so let
me clear your mind up on this… It wasn't really necessary for me
to explain the details of my past troubles and divorce, other than
the fact I'm a single parent." "But when you first told me that you

contracted the virus, my thought was you cheated on me and tried to put it on me knowing that you are…" (Darryl backs away from the couch, and interrupts me to say…)

"A truck driver, right?" "All truck drivers sleep around at every stop they make, right?" "Is that what you're about to say?" "Well, you're wrong, and it's an insult to me and my profession!" Darryl said. "You know what your problem is Cheryl! You stereotype every and anybody that works in my field." (I was speechless, after hearing that from Darryl, because I can admit I'm wrong if it's true…) "I've been open and honest about everything Cheryl!" "I have too Darryl, and I'm sorry for thinking the way I have!" I replied. "I just wanted the truth, and didn't see this coming no more than you did." I pleaded.

After several exchanged words of justification coming between me and Darryl with no solution or real answers, I felt intense emotions of anger inside of me that was about to abrupt I wasn't prepared to happen… "I'm sick and tired of all this and don't know where to turn! I feel I don't deserve what is happening to me!!" I shouted. "Like I told you before, had I known the results of my test, I wouldn't have given you the chance to be part of my life!!" Once I said that, I collapsed to the floor, fluttered in tears and overwhelmed uncontrollable emotions from the constant disappointments and trauma in my life. "Cheryl, Cheryl!" He tried to pick me up… "Leave me alone!" I cried out. "Come on Cheryl, get a grip of yourself, it's not that serious." Darryl said emphatically. Darryl again attempted to pick me up from the floor, then successfully puts me on the couch to calm me down, by wiping the tears from my eyes with his hands... "Cheryl, C'mon baby..." "It's ok calm down you're having a nervous breakdown." "Like I told you before, I'm not going anywhere." "I love you, and we will work this thing out together." Softly, Darryl said.

I managed to catch myself by sitting up to gain my composure, to tell him... "What you don't understand Darryl is I don't want this relationship anymore!" "If I stay with you, I would have to face you everyday living in guilt that I gave you something bad, and destroyed your life because of my ex-husband's doing!" "I cannot forgive or forget what he did to me, therefore I hate him, and if I hate him, it would be difficult for me to love you!" "What was done to me, I wouldn't wish that on my worst enemy so, I don't think it would be good if we continue to see each other anymore... It's over Darryl!" I concluded in tears. The look on Darryl's face was mixed with disbelief and sorrow... "No Cheryl!" He shouted. I quickly moved his arm and hands from me and jumped up from the couch to say... "Yes, It's over Darryl, sorry." "Cheryl, you can't be serious! We've been through too much together, please don't do this!" I knew I have to move quickly before any further feelings of want to try creep up on me so I said... "Darryl, please don't make this any harder on me than it needs to be, you are only hurting the matter more." Darryl jumps up trying to hold my hand in plea to change my mind, but I backed off with my arm stretched out and hands up signaling "Stop!" So, I tell him... "Darryl, it's time to leave." I proceeded to the door and opened it, extending my arm out the door for him to go, while my head was down. He looked at me intensely, and saw that I wasn't changing my mind, but to ask… "For sure?" "Yes Darryl, for sure, bye Darryl." He gave one more look into my face, and then slowly walked out to his car. I shut the door behind him and locked it with a sigh of relief. But came again the tears of a torn wounded woman I was. I leaned my back against the door, then slide down to the floor, to throw my hands up to say "Why me, why me!" All I can think of is where do I go from here and when will this ever end…

CHAPTER 17

Who's fooling Who?
Class Reunion Cont.

"SO, GIRL!" "WHO ELSE IS HERE?" SHEILA ASKED. "I don't know, it seems that we've walked the whole entire room and seen almost everyone we don't know from back in the days." Shemika said. "Oh well, I was hoping to see Trent, to see if he's still sexy and good looking." Sheila said. "I would think so Sheila, he was a track star and most men who love sports would try to keep their shape." "You probably right Shemika." "He's probably busy, owner of a business doing well or something and didn't really have time for class reunions…" "What are you trying to say Shemika?" "We low lives have nothing better to do but to be nosy what other classmates are doing?" "Pretty much Sheila, lol" "Lol, that's funny Shemika probably true in some cases, lol."

"Look, everyone is clapping, let's get back to our seats, some guy is about to say something…" Sheila said. Walking back to the seats, Sheila noticed Roderick wasn't back from getting his drink, but quickly brushed it off because of the announcement that was about to be made… "Good evening Ladies and Gentlemen, welcome to our 10th year class reunion!" Roderick, at the bar after he left the lobby from Trina, now quickly rushes back to sit with Sheila and her friend after hearing the beginning of the speaker's voice, before further announcements. He sat casually next to Sheila, while she momentarily gazed at him to say… "Honey, where have you been?" "Shoot, Sheila! Don't act like you missed me that much, it's you and your girl, I'm just here, remember?" Roderick said sarcastically. "Shut up Rod, smart mouth! Lol" "Yeah, whatever Sheila." He said with a smirk. "Shh! He's about to make an announcement." "Sheila whispered."

"Right now, I'm about to announce the best and worst from our yearbook, and proud to share our past best of the best winners that year 2004 class…" "We had Sarah Jones for best dress, Bobby Whitmore for best dancer, Lela Pearson for most likely to succeed, and last the person who stole the hearts of many women, guess what?" "He is here with us tonight!" The announcer said. The crowd wondered in suspense, wanting to know who this person was… "He was nominated to be the best athlete, a track runner who still to this day holds the school record…"

As soon as both Sheila heard that, they knew already it would be Trent… "Girl! He's talking about Trent!" Sheila said. Roderick, at first was non challan or less enthused of the reunion activities, soon became attentive, realizing it was Sheila's last boyfriend, the announcer was beginning to introduce. "Roderick looked around to see if Trent was sitting in the audience anywhere, but no sight of him. Sheila looked back at Roderick to say… "Are you jealous yet? Lol." Roderick raised his eyebrow for a moment of disbelief as if he couldn't believe what she just said, then looked at Sheila to say… "You're not serious, are you?" "I'm just joking Roderick, don't be so serious! Lol." Sheila said as she rubbed his knee. "You know him as Trent!" As soon as the crowd heard his name called, the room went from quiet to clapping and shouting as if he was a celebrity. "Now, now you ladies! I know that you are excited that he's hears tonight, but allow me to finish the introduction…" "Trent, who was phenomenal on the field and off…" The women with great anticipation, began to jump up shouting for Trent to appear before the announcer had a chance…" "Lol, lol ok ladies, I see now I'm not going to be able to finish the introduction, so allow me to get to the point… You all known him as Trent, but tonight, I introduce to you now Trina!"

From excitement to disbelief, the room suddenly came silent not sure what they just heard. Both Sheila and Shemika were even more shocked of the news… "Girl, did you just hear what he said?" "Yeah Sheila, he said Trina, like he's a woman now!"

When Roderick first heard the name "Trina" he quickly sat up, his demeanor went from calm to panic now that he knows the real reason why Trina was here. His hands became sweaty as if he just splashed water on them. His mind raced with thoughts (what if, Trina tells Sheila I slept with her, or she tells her I have secrets, or maybe she's here to destroys my marriage by confronting me in public…) (Please Trina! Not tonight!).

As soon as the announcements ended and the introduction of Trina, comes this person on stage looking glamorous and adored. All eyes that saw, were on her with mixed reactions from disbelief stunned, to acceptance it was Trent, now a woman, a transvestite, Trina. A woman, who mirrors every feature the feminist character of a woman, shocks the whole ball room in aww… "Oh my god!" Shemika said. "Wow!" Sheila shouted. After the crowd had seen the new Trent from being silent and astonished, to approval with applause, Sheila sat back in amazement of the news, as her eyes continued to be opened wide to the point her eyes seemed ready to fall out of her eye-sockets from the shock of it all. "I can't believe how good Trent looks as a woman!" Sheila said. "I can't believe it either!" Shemika said.

Trina takes the microphone to say… "Hello everyone!" "Yes, it's me Trent now Trina!" "Now don't look so amazed and shocked, I can very well see that you are; It's really me in the new flesh rein-carnated if I may say!" Trina said with a smile. After Trina's speech, people applauded her even more… "Now, if you really like what you see, and want to know what I'm made of, come visit me at my new strip club called "Z's Night Club" located on the strips of Las

Vegas…" "So, that's right! You guessed it! I'm a professional stripper who owns a club." When Sheila and the women reacted to the news Trent now Trina, Roderick stays low key in hopes he's not noticeable for Trina to see, but says to himself… (I can't believe my luck!) (How in the hell did I get myself into this?) (It's about to get out of hand if I don't do something about it.) Sheila proceeds to get up from the table along with Shemika… "Where are you going Sheila?) "I'm going to see if I can catch Trent, oops, I mean Trina before she's leaves!" "Why Sheila? That ain't necessary, I mean do you really have to?" "Rod, calm down, it looks like you don't have to worry about Trent anymore stealing me away, lol"

Both Sheila, Shemika and several women in the ballroom, tried to go talk and meet her after the speech while Roderick sits hoping for the best outcome from any suspicion of Trina's intent. Getting closer to Trina, Sheila's memories of Trent immediately slipped away as she admired Trina's long gold glittered dress, that hugged her entire body with gold expensive high heels to match, she noticed Trina's slightly dyed hair color maroon, that was dressed down to her back, and her face wonderfully made up with make up like she just walked out the beauty parlor. Sheila tapped the shoulder of Trina, to get her attention away from the other women to ask… "Trina! Do you remember me?" Sheila asked. Trina looked back at Sheila with excitement to say… "Excuse me girls, I have some catching up to do with this girl whom I've known way back." The ladies proceeded to walk away to now the attention is between both Sheila and Trina… "Girl of course I do!" "Do you remember I used to call you fine cocoa self?" Trina asked. "Yeah, you did used to call me that, lol." "Now why did you call me cocoa self?" "That's because you were the finest dark chocolate in the school and I had to have you to myself, lol!" Trina said. "I can't believe the changes you've made and how surprisingly, it looks good on you!" Sheila said. "I too must say you came out really good! "Thank you Shemika!" "Blame it on a little surgery and hormone treatment." "I mean the results did work wonders to the point it surprised me too, lol." Trina said. "But your face is not masculine anymore, and your body, hair, and skin complexion made you look like a model or a celebrity for sure, lol." "Thank you, thank you again Shemika for your lovely words…"

"And how is your family doing these days?" "I remembered your brother George, who played basketball at the school. Is he ok?" "He's fine, he went to the Army and after that, became a Pharmacist." "Good for him!" "Make sure that you tell him I said Hi ok!" Trina said. "Most definitely, I will." Shemika said with a smile.

As the girls continued to conversate, Trina looked over at Roderick from afar, enjoying watching him suffer in suspense wondering if she is telling Sheila what's really been going on between her and Roderick, but instead, while she glanced at him, she noticed how Roderick stared intensely back at her to communicate body language with his eyes and lips to say in silence… "Stop it!" So, Trina getting the message ask… "So, Shemika tell me!" "Is anyone here married?" "I'm not, but Sheila is." "I am Trina!" Sheila said. "Oh really?" "As a matter of fact, he's here with me tonight." Sheila responded. "So why don't you come with us to meet him at our table Trina!" "Sure, why not!" Trina said with a smirk. Roderick now panicking, wondering what might come next, taking another shot of his Grey Goose he had left to drink, now notices Trina coming to his table with both Sheila and Shemika… "Roderick!" "Guess who's here with me!" Roderick with barely any eye contact, says… "What's that?" He responded callously. "Not what Roderick, but who… Trent! Now Trina!" "Yeah? And so!" "Roderick, stop being rude and get up by greeting the new lady…lol! Sheila demanded.

Roderick reluctantly got up to extend his hand to say… "What's up with you?" "Roderick! That's not a way to greet a woman!" Sheila said. "Lol, it's ok Sheila, he's a little star struck, lol." "I must say aren't you tall, lol." Trina said. "I mean how do you handle this big hunk in the bedroom Sheila? I can't imagine, lol" After that comment, Roderick stared down Trina to say with his lips in silence… "Quit!" But Trina ignored all his body signs, to continue to torture him in front of Sheila by extending her hand and hold his hand enough to say back in silent lip talk… "Got you now." They immediately sat down for Roderick to ask the question… "So, what made you decide to make this change, if I may ask?" Trina looked at him professionally without any suspicion from Sheila, to say… "I discovered it was already in me to be a woman and didn't know how to bring it out when I was younger. But as time when on, I finally decided to make that move after high school graduation, to become the woman I am today." Trina said. "If you like what you see, come visit me at a location downtown Chicago, my copartner's strip club called, "Ecstasy Lounge" "Wow

Trina! Your business must be doing well." Sheila said. "It is love, and I'm glad about it." "But if your husband like what he sees than maybe I will give him a lap dance for free, lol!" "Ooh, Roderick she just called you out, lol!" Sheila said. Roderick gave no response, but to say in his mind… (Just maybe if you didn't have my wife here tonight!) "We would like that, lol!" Sheila said.

Trina stares a moment at Roderick, wondering what to say next to get him heated… "That's all ladies and gentleman, I must leave now because I have business to take care of, like this man I meant tonight, he wants to meet with me for a drink, lol" Trina said. "Oh, before you go Trina, can we get your number?" Sheila asked. "Sure, let me reach down my purse and give you all my business cards…" As Trina gives out her number, Roderick discreetly shake his head slowly in disagreement to Trina, but she ignored. "So, call me anytime ladies!" "Bye Trina, it was good to meet you!" Sheila said. They all hugged and as Trina was walking away, she looked back at Roderick, and rolled her eyes at him to say to herself… (I got him!) While Trina slowly walked away, Sheila watched Roderick looking down at Trina to say… "You busted!" Roderick panicked for a moment to ask… "Busted? For what?" "For looking at Trina's booty, lol!" Roderick now irritated and disgusted, now ask… "Look, I'm tired, are you ready to go now?" "Calm down Rod!" "I was just joking." Sheila replied. "That wasn't funny Sheila!" "I mean, how do you call yourself asking for her number to stay in touch?" "For what?" "So ya'll could be friends?" "Hell no, it ain't happening!"

Angrily after saying that, Roderick proceeds to get up to head out of the ballroom as Sheila watched… "I guess he didn't like that girl, lol!" Shemika said. "I guess so too, lol!" "Girl, it's late, let me go catch up with cry baby, lol." "I'll call you later ok?" Both Shemika and Sheila hugged as they left. Sheila rushes out the ballroom to the lobby looking for Roderick as he stood near the exit of the hotel waiting, Sheila walks up to him to say… "You've been acting funny all evening since we got here, what's up with you Rod?" "Nothing Sheila, just ready to go!" "If you that paranoid over an old crush having her number, then I'll let it go, satisfied?" Sheila said. Roderick look down at her with approval to say… "Good, now let's go, I'm tired."

During the ride home, Roderick was anti-social as he drove, no eye contact or any gesture to follow that would strike any conversation. Sheila looks from the passenger seat at him with curiosity… "Why are you so quiet Roderick?" "Don't have much to say right now, just tired." Sheila continued to stare, to see if any changes in facial expressions to ask… "Are you jealous?" "Roderick, stunned by the question, to ask… "Jealous of what?" "Trina wanting to stay in touch by giving her card to me, and the fact I used to have a crush on her when she was Trent." "Well, let me correct you on two things: One, it was your idea of staying in touch asking for a number; two, that is not a woman, but a man." "So, I ain't trippin off no thing that can't seem to make up its mind to be a woman or a man." "No competition here when it comes to being a man." He said. "First of all, Rod, she's not a thing but a woman!" "I don't see anything wrong staying in touch." "So, tell me, what's really wrong

Rod?" "What in the hell was you thinking when you told Trina we'll come see you at your club?" "That was stupid for you to even ask that question, knowingly we don't go to strip clubs!" He said vocally. "Ok, ok Rod!" "You're taking this a little too serious all of sudden that makes me wonder what you be doing…" Sheila said as she observed his response… "Tell me the truth Rod, are you ok?"

Roderick, with a straight face as he drives, said… "Yeah, I'm good." "It's just that if we are working on bettering our marriage, then we must focus our attention between us, instead of me looking at other women in that club, you wouldn't want that, would you?" Sheila looked back at him, absorbing all that was said, to say… "Don't act like you got all the sense, but I see what you are saying…" After Sheila made that comment, Roderick now feels that he made a homerun, convincing Sheila's thoughts otherwise to think of him innocent and had an argument good enough for her to accept… "My point is Sheila I don't want you gett'n involved with Trent, Trina, or whatever it trying to be…" "Ok, once again, you win Rod!" "If that's what you want, then so be it!" Sheila laughs. "Thank you!" Roderick replied.

Soon as they arrived home, Sheila's phone ring… "Hello?" "Hey Shemika! What's up girl!!" Roderick thought to himself… (Didn't they just talk not too long ago??…) (My baby looking too good tonight, I'm horny and I know I'm about to get some…) Two hours went by, now settled in bed, the only action happening at that moment is Sheila still on the phone, reminiscing with Shemika, while Roderick looks on wondering when the conversation will end, so he can get busy in love making with Sheila.

Another hour past, Roderick looks on to the ceiling in frustration seeing that his night cap has faded away from phone engagement with Shemika with no sight of end, he soon realizes that his moment of fantasy with Sheila ended. Another hour past now 2:00am in the morning… "Sheila! Will you get off that phone! I'm trying to sleep here!" Roderick shouted. Sheila rolled from having her back turned from him, to now face him, but before she was able to say anything to Roderick, Sheila replied back to Shemika… "What Girl?" "What's that noise?" "That's nothing but hold on Girl…" Sheila place her hand over the phone to whisper to Roderick… "I'll be off the phone in a few minutes, ok." "You said that an hour ago Sheila!" Roderick yelled. "Like I said Roderick, I will be off the phone in a few minutes." Roderick wasn't buying it, so he gets up shaking the bed from frustration to say "Forget this!" Sheila continued her conversation while looking on at Roderick to say… "Hold on Girl!" "Roderick, where are you going?" "To the kitchen away from you to get a cold one!" "Text me when you think you have time for me and permission to return to my own bed and wife!" He slammed the bedroom door behind him, to proceed down the steps to the kitchen to grab a beer.

Now in the kitchen, he reached for his phone that was left on the kitchen counter to see if he had a text yet from Sheila, but instead to find that he had several text messages from Trina reading…" We need to talk." "Look down to see if something is excited after seeing me last night." "When was it the last time I blew your mind?" As Roderick read his messages, he takes big gulps of his beer, so it could relax him and forget he didn't get any attention from Sheila. As the beer took full effect of his thoughts, he began wondering to himself… "This girl is a trip!" "I think she has a real fatal attraction for me." "She doesn't know, it's not about to happen, because I'm going to end this once and for all."

In between thoughts of what he felt what was right, juggled with other thoughts to go back justifying why he should keep seeing her. Clogged in is better judgement now turned into danger signs, not heeding to his conscious, led him into further drifting, sunk in his beers, thinking now… "Man, Trina did look good last night, even better looking than Sheila." "Man, I'm tripp'n, lol!" Roderick takes another sip until noticing another text from Trina saying… "If you are thinking about me, call me now!" Roderick says to himself… "How does she know I'm thinking about her this time in the morning?" "Sometimes I think she must have some spell on me because I can't seem to shake it off!" "What's the use, call her and see what she wants!" "She did look good and smelled good last night, even better than Sheila did." "I'm going to hate myself for this, but I'm going to call her just to chill until I can get my anger down with Sheila not hooking me up. Roderick calls Trina after a couple rings… "What took you so long?" Trina asked. My baad, didn't know I had a time line to call." "Don't get smart with me now, so where is your wife and why are up so late?" Trina asked. "Can't sleep because my wife is on the phone talking to her girlfriend Shemika!" "Lolol, so let me guest, your wife is not attending to her wifely duties by being on the phone all night, leaving you helpless with no one to rescue you of your needs." "So, you decided to call me in hopes I can rescue you in your dire need, right, lol!" Trina said. "Ok genius, you win!" Roderick said. "So, when are you going to make up your mind and stop playing games with me with your emotions." "You've told me many times you like this, and your wife doesn't even come close satisfying you like I do." "So, quit the ..." "Hold it Trina!" Roderick quickly catches himself after raising his voice enough for Sheila to hear from downstairs, so he covers the phone to peak toward the stairs where the bedroom door insight to listen for any noises of Sheila talking... (yeah, yeah girl and then...)

Roderick hears that she's still on the phone, feeling even more frustrated, gives full attention back to Trina... "Look Trina, I told you the last time I will hook up with you, so stop sweating me!" "Ok Mr. Roderick, when will that be? When I finally have a baby?" "Don't play stupid with me now Trina." "Hey, by the way, you think you could... "No Roderick!" "I'm not having phone sex with you, to fulfill your fantasies, until you come through for me!" "We've been playing this game too long now, and it's about me this time." "Ok Trina, I 'll get with you this weekend for sure – I promise." "Fine then, in the meantime, I'll go back to Craigslist and see who I can hook up with." Trina said. "No damnit! Roderick hollered by accident, but quickly again checks to see if the bedroom light under the closed door is on and to hear any noises of Sheila on the phone... (Good, I think Sheila is finally asleep) "Hey Trina, like I said, I got you and will try to see you tomorrow and this weekend... Satisfied now?" "Will see." Trina said. "As a matter of fact, you need to take your profile off Craigslist for good!" Roderick demanded. "Whoa, what are you saying? You got claims to this?"

Trina asked. "Look, just do what I said, and I'll talk with you later... Gotta go!" "Bye!"

Roderick hangs up the phone. A few minutes later went by for Roderick to notice a text that read... "We'll see who really got claims to who..."

CHAPTER 18

Hidden Enemy – Trouble at Work

IT HAS BEEN A COUPLE OF MONTHS, SINCE I'VE HEARD back from Darryl, and probably the longest since our breakup. I took courage to get treated for the HIV where it is manageable in my day to day life. Focused as a single parent, I gained strength to take Michael back to court for full custody of Sabrina while finally receiving child support from his checks. I probably could had handled my stress from Michael to Darryl better if my mother was still here to comfort me with her love and wisdom.

I can remember long ago she would have many talks with me on her dying bed of breast cancer in the hospital, but it was this one conversation I would always remember… "Trust God my child whether it be good or bad." "He will get you through it all with triumph!" For some reason, that thought would come at the right time when I needed it most. Now at work with a clear mind, focused on my work at hand with patients, I knew it was appraisal time, especially for me, since I applied for the open position as head nurse. But while at work, I've noticed Kim at her desk punching away on the computer, while others walked pass me did not say hi, but just looked at me as they went by, of course I didn't care about all that because sooner or later, they would be reporting to me. I picked up a male patient's record, to proceed to his room, to see if he's doing fine, but when I looked at my folder, I realized I picked up the wrong folder for the room so… "Kim, I need your help!" "Hold on Cheryl I'm coming!" "What's up?" Kim asked. "I just realized that I picked up the wrong folder and I got two patients in room 102 that supposed to get IV attended to them, would you please take care of that for me while I attend to this patient?" "Not a problem Cheryl!" "Thanks!" I turned my head back to the patient I was attending to until… "Mr. Wilmington! Why are you looking at me in that way?" "Are you thinking nasty thoughts again?" "No, no Ms. Cheryl, lol" "I was just admiring you, lol."

Although Mr. Wilmington may seem to be a nice guy, he can most certainly be flirtatious without hesitation, thinking he still has it. I see that he graced handsomely in his old age with freckles on his head and face, I can tell that he used to be a light skinned young guy with red hair, it's no wonder to him to think he still has it. I can tell that he was a lady's man back in his days, and ability to woo the women of his time, but with me, not today. "I look at you because you're so beautiful, and I cannot keep my eyes off of you." Mr. Wilmington said. "Well unfortunately Mr. Wilmington, you have to close them in order to get much needed rest after that long bypass surgery." "I know Ms. Cheryl, but you are the only one who can make me sleep better." He said. I stood back and smiled to ask… "Now why is that Mr. Wilmington?" "Because it seems like you really care about me, and it makes me feel good!" He replied. "Aww, that was very nice of you to say, but you really must rest now!" I rubbed his shoulder and tucked him under his sheet until… "Cheryl! Ms. Pritchard wants to see you immediately in her office. I looked up at Kim from having a peaceful moment with my patient Mr. Wilmington, to fully alarmed at the reaction from Kim delivering the message… "Is everything ok Kim? You look like you were running out of breath just to tell me, lol!" "I don't know girl but it may be good or bad, but just be prepared."

From the looks in her eyes told me it may not be good, but what she doesn't know is I applied for the position as head nurse, and my appraisal is up for review, so I will surprise her after the meeting. "Ok, I'm on my way." I said. As I approached Ms. Pritchard's office, I can tell that she was expecting my arrival anytime soon as she looked up between the blinds of her office to see me coming, but she quickly lowered her head to continue reading whatever was in front of her wearing bi-focal glasses glaring from the reflection of the light and paperwork illuminating her glass focal to the point you couldn't tell if she was looking up at you or still studying paperwork before her… I Knocked on the door, she looked up to signal with her hand come in… I opened the door to say "Ms. Pritchard, you wanted to see me?" "Yes, please sit down and close the door." She said with sternum in her voice.

I sat down in front of her desk, notice her demeanor was cold and no eye contact. As I looked upon her face, I see bushy hair like she must had worked all night with no sleep, but well neat and organized in her work and office. I say to myself… (Boy, with all that money she makes, you would think she would hire a hair stylist to keep up with all that hair, lol) "Cheryl, as you may know that the hospital do appraisals without merit, and randomly call personnel in to evaluate their performances, right?" "Yes Ms. Pritchard, I am aware of this." "Good!" "Well, your name came up on my desk so guest what? It's your review time!

Now in my years of experience conducting this task, it's been painful and most time pleasing. In your case, let's hope for the best." Ms. Pritchard said with a smile. "Yes Ms. Pritchard, I hope so too." "I'm looking at your file, and I must say that upon reviewing it, I'm pleased at your performances." "I was impressed at the sacrifice and commitment showed in your work to be extraordinary and exceptional." "Thank you, Ms. Pritchard!"

"In your field of profession, you've demonstrated and upheld integrity in your work and care for the patience needs; you've sustained the values and principles of this hospital, even in direst situations." "You've showed good ethics and great character that to me, warrants you the opportunity for a higher position."

After hearing all this coming from her, I was expecting her to tell me that I got the promotion and to say that I will be the next head nurse until… "However, there is one thing that's troubling me about this whole evaluation…" "What's that Ms. Pritchard?" "As you may know that the hospital requires that I review all medical records of every employee in your field, prior to further considerations for promotion, to assure that the decision is the right decision." "It was brought to my attention that a report indicated you've recently contracted STD or HIV without informing proper channels, which puts both staff and patience at risk in the event should you get hurt and someone unwarily comes in contact with your blood, and holds the hospital liable for your actions."

"Therefore, it is my unfortunate duty to place you on leave of absence effective immediately, with pay for the next 90 days, until the board concludes its investigation." "Now heaven forbids, should there have been any reports of patients contracting STD from your negligence, you would probably be facing more repercussions, if not criminal at this time." "But since that's not the case, and because of mitigating factors of your case, the board agreed to place you on leave of absence until further notice." "Now, should their investigation conclude any sooner, you will be notified at that time." Ms. Pritchard concluded. "So, does that mean I'm fired?"

I asked. Ms. Pritchard took her glasses off in a moment of sigh to say… "Cheryl, I probably be looking for another job, but not in the medical field if you want me to be blunt with you." "Sorry!" "Are there any more questions?" "Yes, I wanted to at least explain my actions…" "While I was out for a couple of days, I was very well prepared to report my medical records at that time, until I had an unforeseen situation at home that made me depressed and lost.

So, upon my return, I was prepared to make a report, but to see the report made it to you before I had a chance." I justified. "Ms. Cheryl, you also know that these types of report must be turned in within 48 hours of notification of your results, right?" I put my head down knowing she was right to say… "Yes Ma'am, you are right." "But Ms. Pritchard, I want you to know that I do under-stand the severity of this, and I'm not taking it lightly." "I love my job and the work that I do." I had no intentions of hurting anyone or putting them in danger, so please have some considerations…" I said tearfully. But Ms. Pritchard wasn't moved by it to say… "I need you to turn in your keys and access cards immediately after clearing out your desk and locker ok?" Ms. Pritchard demanded. "Please Ms. Pritchard don't do this to me, not now!" Sadly, I got up tearfully, to walk out her office, for her to say… "Have a nice day!" I said to myself (You just fired me to say something as stupid as that? How unthoughtful she is!) Feeling lost with shame and embarrassed, you might as well shoot me now, it might feel better than what I'm feeling now.

CHAPTER 19

Who's Fooling Who? –
Fears revealed

TWO MONTHS LATER… "SHEILA, THANKS FOR STAYING over after service." "You are welcome Pastor!" "I called you in my office for several reasons…" "One is to commend you on your consistent attendance here at the church; secondly, I'm a little concerned for my son, as to why he hasn't returned any of my calls, and not showing up in services with you these last couple of months." "Is there a problem or concern I need to be aware of?" He asked. "Not really Pastor." "Roderick has been under a lot of pressure with his job since their numbers been down. He's been working a lot of hours to help bring their numbers up." Sheila justified. Roderick's father, the Pastor, leans back in his chair, while studying Sheila's face like a father would at his child, and asked… "Are you ok?" "Do you need anything from me?" "No Pastor, I mean father, lol" "It's ok Sheila, I sometimes have to remember to change roles from pastor to now father, lol" "I'm fine for now, but I am a little surprised to hear that Roderick hasn't been returning your calls."

Now assured from his daughter-in-law Sheila… "Let me know if I can be of help with anything." "No problem father, and thank you for caring." Sheila said. They both got up and hugged each other with departing words… "Hopefully, I'll see you both soon in service." "I hope so too father, bye!" Sheila left out his office heading towards outside to reach down her purse as she walked, for her phone to call Roderick… (Phone rings…) "Hey it's me! Give me a call back as soon as you get this message."

Sheila thinks and ask herself (Why isn't he picking up and what is he doing that is more important than my calls?) (He's at the house so there's no excuse for not picking up!) Minutes later, Sheila hits redial as she is driving… "Hello!" "Why didn't you pick up earlier Rod when I called?" "I did pick up, but you hung up on me." Roderick justified. "Ok, if that's true then why didn't you call back?" Sheila asked. But Roderick didn't answer but instead, he asked… "So, what's up?" "I just left the church, talking with your father in his office telling me you haven't returned his calls and wants to know if you were alright." "What did you tell him?" "I told him you were working late and didn't have time."

As Sheila continued to talk to Roderick, she soon realized to herself and say in her mind (Why am I protecting him, for he is a grown man who can speak up for himself!) "Anyway, why are you ignoring his calls?" "It's like you said, I've been busy, even you should know that!" "Rod, why are you getting an attitude with me?" "Because, I know you Sheila!" "You probably sat there agreeing with everything my father said bad about me." "What are you talking about Rod?" "You're not making any sense what you're saying!" Sheila suspected something was wrong in his speech... "Have you been drinking again Rod?" There was silence on the other end as Roderick did not respond... "I tell you what Rod, you continue by ignoring me, while you drown yourself in the alcohol until you fall out like you normally do!" "Bye!"

After hanging up, Sheila said to herself as she continued driving to say... "Rod hasn't been right ever since the class reunion two months ago." "All we do is fuss and fight over nothing." "He acts like his father and the world is against him including me." "I mean we haven't had sex in a month." "Every time I tried to go there with him, he makes excuses why he's not in the mood." "That's not like him to turn me down." "He's making me wonder if he's seeing someone else..." "He must be, because as horny he gets all the time, it would be strange that he didn't want it." But in her thinking, she tried to rationalize his actions by saying... "Wait a minute me!" "He's been working late so he could had been really tired." "Well, whatever it is, I'm going to have a talk with him as soon as I get home, but before I do, I'm trashing any alcohol left in that house, because I think the alcohol is messing with him and his thinking which is now out of control!" "Wait until I get to the house!"

CHAPTER 20

Hidden Enemy – Truth Comes out

AFTER HEARING THAT I WAS ON LEAVE OF ABSENCE from the job, I walked out of Ms. Pritchard's office feeling defeated, mixed with emotions of anger amongst sadness. I still couldn't get over her last comment "Have a nice day." I said to myself screw her and her day, because she just messed up mines. I tried to keep my composure and head down as I left her office without notice, but unsuccessfully, people around me stopped and looked with mixed feelings of sympathy, oblivious of what just happened but to look to see what my reaction would be as if they knew already, and this one person that smiled at me at my worse moment, to think maybe she knew and had something to do with it… "What are you looking at heffer?" "You got something to say? Then say it now!" I shouted unexpectantly. But she didn't respond but turned her face away. Never did liked her in the first place, because she's nothing but a backstabber!

As I continued to walk, I felt the need to hurry out of their presence, but my feet couldn't move any faster from the news that blew me away. But I managed to roll my eyes at each one that did not show empathy for me. Finally, I'm at my locker to take off my scrubs to further realize since leaving Ms. Pritchard's office, no one said nothing to help console me, not even a single word of comfort. Because of their silence, it made me angrier and more upset to discover folks at the hospital were not my friends after all. "Ya'll can quit pretending like you didn't know what just happened, because ya'll phony and could not keep it real with me!!" I shouted.

After that, I looked over at my locker to see its now empty except the picture of my mother and I posing at my graduation from medical school, I began to cry again while holding my left hand to my mouth, and right hand to slowly reach for the last thing in my now past locker to say… "Mama where are you when I need you most!" "God help me please!" I said with tears. Once again, I could hear my mother say… "Trust God, he will get you through with triumph."

Now outside struggling with the things in my hand trying to reach for my keys feeling defeated, shaken, and traumatized all over again, I reached for my car door until someone startled me from behind with a tap on my shoulder… "Cheryl! Long time no see." "Now before you say anything, just want you to know I've been trying to reach you for the longest, but you wouldn't answer my phone calls nor call back. I left several messages on your door in attempt to see you but… "Darryl! Why would you come here to my job?" I interrupted. "Suppose if I was busy!" "How dare you even come here to cause trouble while I'm at work!" "Baby please no!" "I didn't come here for all that." "I'm not your baby anymore

Darryl!" "Ok, ok Cheryl, just listen to me for a moment." "I came here to see you and to tell you something very important you need to know." "In light of what all has happened between us and my job here in Houston, I accepted a better position in my hometown Portland, Oregon, as a local driver that pays more where my medical condition is irrelevant to them." "Well congratulations Darryl on your new found success, so have a good life!" (I said sarcastically) "I must go now." I said.

I turned away to reach for my car door until Darryl stopped me to say… "Wait a minute!" "There's one more thing…" "I also came to tell you I still love you and I want you to quit your job and come with me." (I stopped what I was doing and looked at him to ask…) "Now why on earth would I do that when I live here?" "Look Cheryl, it's like this, after our last conversation, I knew then you were telling me the truth and wouldn't do me any harm to destroy me." "You didn't know and it's not your fault." "it is what it is, and that's why I'm here." He places my boxes and stuff into my car, then gets on one knee, and when I saw what was about to happen, I couldn't help myself but to start crying overwhelmed, that this man loves me that much for better or worse! "Marry me Cheryl! I want you to be my wife!" "But, before you answer, take this…" Darryl handed over a small purple bag, my favorite color, because he knew I loved "Prince" in "Purple Rain" with a purple bow on it. Inside was a purple small box… "Open it honey!" Darryl said. So, I opened it to discover a 2-carat single diamond encrypted with our initials inside "D.C." "A ring Darryl? Really?" As I stood there in aww from the ring and proposal, Darryl still on his knee waits for an answer… "So, honey will you marry me?" I couldn't answer him because I was too surprised and adored the ring while playing with it on my finger to see if it fit correctly, forgetting that Darryl asked a question, at least twice, he gets up and looks at me, but before he could say anything I kissed him intensely until he slowly moved his lips away from mines to say… "I take that as a yes!" I grabbed him to kiss him again and to say… "Yes, baby yes!"

I knew that I felt the same way as he did, but the reason why I broke up with him in the first place, is because I didn't want him to throw it in my face that it was me who gave him the virus on purpose. "Now baby, you don't have to rush to marry me if you don't want…" "Boy quit playing!" "You knew what you came here for." "But I must say, it was a bold move for you to do what you did." "I'm glad you did, because you made my day." "I did?" (Of course, he doesn't know what I went through today, so I will share the details later) "Yes! You did! So, follow me home, I will tell you something what happened today when we get there." We kissed, got into our separate cars, and headed home. While driving, I think again what my mother said and now I see it. My day went from bad, to worst, then changed to be good. While driving, I occasionally would look at my left hand, wearing something I have not seen in a long time, a ring that shows that Darryl truly loves me no matter what! I'm wearing the bling bling, lol! A call comes in… "Hello!" "Cheryl!" "Where are you?" Kim asked. "Girl, you don't know?" "They let me go!" "What!" "Are you serious?" "What do you mean they let you go?" Kim asked. "They put me on administrative leave for 90 days!" "90 days for what Cheryl?" "Ms.

Pritchard found out that I contracted STD, the HIV virus." "But how did she find out?" "I really don't know Kim." "She claimed that it came up on my medical records and it came back showing that I've been test positive for STD, and that would put the hospital at risk." I said. "That's crazy, I mean how would they have known that so soon." "Aren't you mad about it?" "Right now, I don't want to think about it, because so much has happened today." "Well, I went by your desk and noticed everything was gone, so I knew than, something was wrong." "That's why I'm calling you now!" Kim said.

"So, how are you holding up Cheryl?" "I'm ok for now, but guest what happened after I left the hospital?" "What Cheryl?" "After leaving the hospital, Darryl was outside standing by my car to propose to me, to marry him!" I said. "What? For real!" Kim said with excitement. "Yes Girl, and he gave me a 2-Karat ring that is on my finger right now!" "Wow Girl, I'm happy for you!" Kim said. While driving, with Darryl following me, I continued to share the details with Kim until she said… "Hold on Cheryl! I got a call coming in!" We paused for a second for her to come back to say… "Hey Cheryl! That's Ms. Pritchard calling me, gotta go… Bye!" Before I was able to say bye back, she hung up the phone. For a moment, I was puzzled, but went back to admiring the ring, and how Darryl proposed to me. Now back at home with Darryl, I shared the good news with Sabrina, and she was happy for us, so, we later that evening we celebrated the news over dinner at a restaurant nearby, followed by later that night, Darryl and I celebrated in our own way in intimacy too deep, even for the wildest imagination I could not put into words. But hopefully, the honeymoon would be the same, if not better.

That morning, I got up, to get ready to prepare bacon, scrambled eggs, grits, and wheat toast with grape jelly, the way Sabrina likes breakfast for the three of us, I go downstairs to realize that I left my purse on the kitchen counter with my cell phone, so I reached to see if any messages, to see 4 missed calls: 2 from Gina, 1 from Kim, and 1 from Jenkins and Smith Law firm… "Who is Jenkins and Smith Law firm?" I asked myself. But before I was able to retrieve the message, a call comes in from the firm. At first, I began to wonder in my mind (maybe someone at the hospital caught the virus, and it's my fault, and they are coming to get me or sue me?) I asked fearing the worst… "Hello?" "Ms. Robertson?" "Yes, how can I help you?" "What is this call concerning?" I asked frantically. My name is Paul Schultz, I'm a legal consultant for Jenkins and Smith Law firm, calling to inform you of a Will Testament, written in the name of "Cheryl Robertson" and "Sabrina Robertson" …" (Now feeling puzzled, who in the family might have a will they forgot to tell me about?) "A will? From who?" "Ma'am, your late husband Michael." (At first, it didn't register in my head that he was talking about Michael, because I was still thinking who would make time to write a will in my name…) "Michael is dead?" "Yes Ma'am, he's deceased." "When did this happen?" (Now I'm beginning to feel like a wife all over again who just lost her husband, don't ask me why, I don't even know…) "He passed away last month from complications…"

(Now I'm beginning to feel sorrow for Sabrina, because I wouldn't know where to begin to tell her father's passing away.)

"I'm sorry Ma'am, our condolences to you and your family, we thought that you knew." Paul, the Lawyer said. "So, please tell me about this Will and why wasn't I aware of this before?" I asked. "Well, this "Will" originated from a gentleman by the name of Larry, the late Mr. Larry Robertson, does that name sound familiar to you?" "Yes, that's Michael's father." "Correct!" He said. "Mr. Larry Robertson, was a wealthy person, who left a Will for Michael, but because of their estranged relationship, his father didn't have any information on him, or his whereabouts." "So, with what little information we had on him, it became an eight-year project for us to find next of kin." "We've managed to find Michael on his death bed prior to passing, for him to make revisions to the Will, and that's how we were able to contact you." "Now I know you may have a lot of questions, and we will be happy to answer them all, but because of the sensitive details and propriety of the Will, I cannot do it over the phone, it's a private matter." "Is it possible for you and your daughter to come to the office tomorrow and meet in person?" "Yes, yes we can!" (At this point, I don't know what to think.

It's beginning to sound like something on tv I seen once before …) "Great!" He said. "What time tomorrow?" I asked. "How about 9:00am tomorrow." "That's too early for me, but can it be 11:00am instead?" "That's fine, 11:00am sharp." "So, what's the address?" "The address is…" (I'm too excited at what I'm hearing, don't even have anything to write down the address, lol) "Hold on Sir, let me get a pen and paper to write with…" "Ok, what's the address?" "It's 1900 Olivia Rd, Suite 16, in the heart of downtown Houston." "Got it?" He asked. "Yes! I got it, thank you!" "We look forward in seeing you!" He said. We hung up. Before I was able to absorb all that has happened, comes another call and its Gina. I rub my face and scratched my head in frustration to say to myself (when will I be able to make breakfast when all these calls keep coming in…)

"Hello!" "Hey Cheryl what's up!" "Why haven't you returned my calls?" Gina asked. "Don't make me have to come over the and mess you up!" Gina said. "Wait a minute Gina, before you decide to go ninja on me, I got to tell you that I just got off the phone, to find out that Michael died." Gina paused for a second than said… "Michael? You mean your ex Michael?" "Yes, that Michael." "When did this happen Cheryl?" "I just found out from this lawyer I hung up with, that he died from the Aids he had last month." "Wow Cheryl! I didn't know it was that serious." (I tell you this Girl may be street wise and tough, but sometimes she can be slow in the head and talk way too much…) "Yes, it was, and the lawyer called to inform me that he left an inheritance or Will for Sabrina!" "Inheritance? What inheritance?" "You mean Michael had some money and didn't tell you about it?" Gina asked. "He didn't know Gina, until the last days of his life, that his father left him something I don't know, and he signed it over to me before he died." "Wow Girl! It better be some money, because he owes us, and if it's a lot a money, you know to hook up yo sista, lol!" (I threw up my arms wondering what did she mean by that…)

"Gina, what do you mean by us?" "Yeah Girl, he owes us, because I call it emotional distress order." "What's that supposed to mean, and what does that have to do with you Gina?" "Shoot Girl, that means he stressed me out hearing that my sista was on an emotional roller coaster and about to go crazy, and stressed out hearing about it…!" "How is it that you were stressed by this when you were locked up in prison?" "Common Cheryl!" "I did get letters in the mail from you, crying all over the pages, and how I knew that, because you left stains of tears that smeared some the letters on the paper, and how he treated you, lol!" "Gina, let it be known, you stupid Girl and crazy for real, lol!" "You, know I'm just trying to lookout for you Cheryl, lol!" "I'm yo big sista, who knows when you're having men trouble, like with Darryl…" "Oh, I almost forgot to tell you Gina what else happened yesterday!" (I can hear the long sigh from Gina on the other end of the call, expecting more bad news, but…) "Oh, Cheryl what now!" "First, the job laid me off, suspended me from work for 90 days." "Suspended why Cheryl?" "You were one of their best nurses, how could that be?" (Oh, I can hear Gina now getting all worked up again…) "Dang Girl! I don't know how much I can take of this! I mean you having HIV, you lost Michael and Darryl, now your job, what more can happen? I need a smoke and a drink, wait…" (This girl is a trip, lol!) "Gina! Come back, not done yet!" "Ok, I'm back!" "What are you drinking this early in the morning anyway?" "Oh girl, got me some vodka…" "Ok, I'm ready, tell me the rest…" Gina said.

"They suspended me for hiding medical records from them about my clinic testing showing positive for HIV." "You just took the test not long ago, how did they find out you had it, and how did they know you took the test again for it to show up on their records?" Gina asked. "I don't know Gina, but they have it." "Last meeting, I had with my boss said I was eligible for promotion to be head nurse, but because of her findings, it costed my job." "Ain't no way Cheryl they would had known about that, unless someone told on you!" (This girl may be slow at times, but like I said, she's street wise, she may have a point!) "Whatever Gina, it still doesn't change the fact my medical career may be over with." "Damn Girl! Sorry to hear that!" "Well enough of that, the second news is Darryl proposed to me and gave me a 2-Karat diamond ring!" (I hear a moment of silence to now shouting constantly from screaming to clapping and words I cannot understand from all the screaming...) "Cheryl, aww yes, ahh, Cheryl, you did that thing!!!" (I think she made had too much to drink...) "When Girl!" "Yesterday Gina, like I said before, it happened right outside the parking lot, just after the bad news with the job." "He said that it didn't matter who got the disease first, he still loves me and wants me as his wife." "Girl, that's what's up! That's a real man for you!" Gina said. "Yes Gina, and he also told me that he found a better job in his hometown Portland, Oregon, and wants Sabrina and I, to move with him." "You might as well Cheryl, since he will be the only one working." "That's not true Gina!" "I'm sure that I will find something else to do out there." (As we continued to talk, I've noticed the clock on the wall said "10:33am" and I've been on the phone for over an hour with no breakfast in sight, and I can hear footsteps of someone walking upstairs, which means I need to hurry up...) "Ok Gina, let me go and get ready for the day, I got breakfast to make for the family!" "Ok Girl, don't forget to give me my share of that money coming to you, remember, I had to read messed up letters from your tears, lol!" "Don't worry Gina, I will make sure that you get a new pad with no tears, lol!" "Bye!"

As I was preparing breakfast, I just remembered to give Kim a call back, but she didn't answer, so I didn't leave a message, because so much to do this morning. The next day at the downtown multi-level parking building, where the law firm is located, now parked, I'm sitting in the car with all kinds of thoughts, not knowing what to expect. Is it a big inheritance like a house, a car, money, or deeds, I don't know. I've never had to deal with a Will before, my family never had much to obtain a Will to give to their love ones, so I don't know where to begin or how to present myself. I'm wearing a business suit in a skirt matching top, white professional blouse in pin stripe grey suit, looking like an attorney my own self, that way I don't stand out different from anyone else. But in my mind, I'm so far distant of what to expect and how to talk professionally at their level. I'm scared and nervous and need something to calm me down. I reached in my purse and remembered I had a wine cooler "Moscato" left from a gathering I had with Kim recently, to quickly drink it, and put some gum after in my mouth, to tone down any alcohol smell. I grabbed my purse to get out the car, to proceed to the elevators.

As I waited for the elevator to push the button, I observed the parking structure full of luxury cars parked, probably from people who are well off, like this firm I'm going to. I began to imagine to myself (I like that red SUV Mercedes, must get one like it after this payoff.) Silly me, I don't even know how much it might be, lol. Now relaxed, the elevator door opens, no one inside but me. I get to the 16th floor where the elevator doors open, I walked out into this beautiful lobby, that looks like a big foyer to a mansion, with beige looking marble floors with black designs shaped diamond. I see the sign on the wall where the receptionist sat that said "Jenkins and Smith Law Firm" I was greeted by the receptionist… "Hello Ma'am, welcome to Jenkins and Smith Law Firm! Who are you hear to see?" This young beautiful blond Caucasian Lady had the prettiest smile, she reminds me of someone from a commercial trying to sell real estate, lol. "I'm here to see Mr. Paul Schultz!" "And your name Ma'am?" "My name is Cheryl Robertson!" "Just a moment Ms. Robertson, I will alert him of your presence, please take a seat, he will be with you in a moment." The receptionist said. I take a seat, hoping the smell of alcohol has ceased from my breath, I looked at my cell phone to see any calls, but to see a text from Darryl wishing me well on this visit.

I looked up to see this Caucasian gentleman, who was well professional looking in his dark solid blue suit with red tie, white shirt as if he was running for office, mid age looking with a great manicured beard… "Hello Ms. Robertson, Cheryl Robertson?" I get up to greet him to say… "Yes! That's me!" "Hi, I'm Paul Schultz, we talked over the phone, glad you made it in!" He said. "Is your daughter here to be with us?" "No, I didn't think she would understand the proceedings, she still getting over the loss of her father." "I can understand that, follow me to a conference room where we can discuss matters."

While in the conference room getting ready to go over the paperwork, Mr. Schultz was very kind in his presentation and made sure that I understood the proceedings in detail. "Would you like something to drink Ms. Robertson?" He asked. "No thank you!" (Little does he know, I just had one, lol) I'm sitting at this long conference table with this man, who has a lot of legal paperwork binder in several expensive looking black leather folders. He opens one of them as he sits across from me… "Now Ms. Robertson, what I have before you are instructions in order to release this Will to next to kin, do you have any questions before I begin?" He asked. (I'm getting nervous, because he's dragging it, not getting to the point! Just hit me with a one or two, so we can knock this out!) "No, I don't." "Once again, we thank you for coming to bring closure to our search next to kin." "I understand this meeting can be difficult for you and your family." "Once we complete this meeting and sign all necessary documents, you are free to disclose any and all information at your discretion to anyone." He said. (I'm getting more anxious, wanting to know exactly what did Michael's father leave and why is this proceeding so necessary…) "As I explained before, your Father-in-law's relationship was distance with your late husband Michael, his son."

"Mr. Larry, so happened to have won the lottery in his town back in 2001 that was worth $63.1 million dollars from a pot he had to split between two other people that left him 17.2 million after taxes." (You should had seen how big my eyes widen after hearing that news…) "Ok, go on please!" I asked. "After spending some of his earnings, he wasn't able to enjoy the rest of it, which is why he decided to distributed the rest of his earnings to his 4 children…" He said. "You mean to tell me Michael had siblings?" "I thought Michael was the only child? He never told me of this!" (This is getting crazier by the moment.) "Yes, he has a total of 4 children including Michael." "Ok, so what does this mean to me?" "It means you will receive $3.4 million dollars, and a full college tuition for your daughter Sabrina." "Any questions?" He asked. (He looked at me expecting that I would jump up or shout in excitement, but instead I was shocked to the point feeling faint…) "Ms. Robertson are you ok?" "Someone get Ms. Robertson some water quickly!!" He shouted out the door conference room.

A few days later after breaking the news to everyone about the inheritance including Kim, I sat back and remembered an old preacher used to say at one time… "God gives you double for your trouble." I certainly received that and thanked him for that." A year later now settled in Portland Oregon, married and now 6 months pregnant, expecting Darryl's first child, I'm in the kitchen getting ready to prepare breakfast for Darryl and Sabrina on a Saturday morning… "What are you doing?" "What am I doing?" I asked. "It looks like I'm getting ready to prepare breakfast!" "Hush, hush my dear lady!" "That's my job and I've already prepared breakfast for you and the family, that is waiting in the sun room!" (I keep forgetting we hired a part-time chef, lol) "Oh, I'm sorry Bruno, lol!" "I keep forgetting we have our own chef!" "It's ok Mrs. Johnson!" "It's not every day that you forget, lol" "You are the bomb Bruno!" I said. "No Mrs. Johnson, you say Hell yea, Bruno is the bomb! Lol! He said "Hell yea Bruno is the bomb! Lol!"

I said. Looking at the breakfast he made, it was picture perfect; He made this chopped seasoned grilled chicken omelet with onions and bell pepper I like, with both white and yellow melted cheese over it, and I must say it again… "Hell yea Bruno is the bomb!!"

As Bruno, the chef prepared to pour the drinks amongst me, Darryl, and Sabrina, we made a toast to each other on our happy life together… "Ma'am, your phone is ringing…" Bruno said. "Hold on everyone, let me take this call…) "I hope it's not your sister Gina again, she already threatens to beat me up if I don't treat you right, lol" Darryl said. "I suggest you duck Darryl if she comes, lol!" "Hold on let me get this call…" "Hello!" (The caller was silent for a moment until…) "Hello Cheryl?" "Yes, who is this calling?" "Cheryl, I'm calling to give you heads up you might be interested in hearing." The caller said. "Heads up on what? Who is this?" "I'm calling to tell you that your girlfriend Kim set you up!" "What are you talking about?" "And how did you get this number?" Darryl looks over at me, to see my facial expressions of worry and confusion to tap me gently on the shoulder to say "Honey, take the call in another room…" I nodded in agreement by getting up to go to the guest room nearby and shut the door… "Who is this again and how did you get this number!" "I starred 69 on Kim's phone your number after she hung up with you, after she framed you." The caller said. "Framed me how?" "I was listening to everything said about you and how Kim betrayed you by telling Ms. Pritchard the real reason why you took off and that you tested positive for HIV and where you went to get tested." "But why would Kim do that to me and what makes you think I would believe that if she's my best friend?" "You don't have to believe me except this… remember you was applying for that head nurse position?" "Yes, I do." "She now has it instead of you!" "But how can I prove all this to be true?" I asked. "Look, I gave you all that you need, just be prepared for what else is coming down against you!" "Against me? Like what? And again, who is this??" "I'm the woman who smiled at you, and you called me a heffer after leaving Ms. Pritchard's office." Click! (She hung up on me…) I asked… "How could she do this to me?

Why would Kim do this to me after all we went through together!" "I thought we were best friends for life!" I cried. (As I sat on the bed in disbelief of our guest room, another call comes…) "Hello!" "Ms. Cheryl Robertson?" "Yes, who is this?" "This is detective Gerald Cruz of the Houston Police Department, Homicide Division, calling on behalf of Houston Medical, we have some concerning questions I need to ask you." "I'm listening…" "There was a death in one of your patients, cared under you prior to your departure, and I need to get some information from you." "I'm going to need you to come down to our station, in order to get some answers, if you fail to appear or cooperate with us, there can be some legal implications behind this that includes charges against you, so do I have your undivided attention?" "Ma'am?" "I can't hear you, say something!" (Kim, it's not over yet! You will pay for this, I promise!!

To be continued!

CHAPTER 21

Who's Fooling Who? –
Judgement Day

SHEILA NOW ARRIVED HOME FROM CHURCH, TO discover Roderick was nowhere to be found but the TV on and remnants of chips and empty spilled beer on the couch. "Roderick where are you!" She shouted across the living room. She began to clean up the mess left from Roderick, turned the TV off, and proceeds upstairs in search for Roderick. "Where are you Rod!" "Answer me!" She shouted. Going towards the master bedroom, assuming that he may be in the bathroom or something, passes their guest room but her eyes caught a body on the floor as she continued to walk, but stopped in her tracks to back up to confirm what she actually saw to discover Roderick laying on the floor knocked out… "Roderick!" Assuming that he was in trouble, Sheila panicked and quickly hurried to him, kneeling down to the floor to his aid, to discover his mouth opened wide from the stench smell of alcohol on his breath… "This fool is drunk and passed out!" She lifted his head up and tried smacking lightly his face… "Roderick, wake up!"

No response from Roderick, so she left him there to further clean up the mess he left on the floor in the guest room. As she was throwing away the emptied beer cans, she noticed the computer was still on… "No, not again! He's been looking at porn!" To close out the website, she noticed in detail what site he was in… Transvestites having sex… Sheila closed out the sites he left, and slammed the laptop screen down, to look over at Roderick on the floor to see that he's still knocked out to say… "How could you Roderick!" "Wait until I tell your father how faithful you really been! She shouted.

A vibration noise goes off nearby the computer, Sheila took her attention off of Roderick, who still knocked out on the floor, to investigate the noise nearby the computer, it's his cellphone behind the computer steady ringing… Sheila picks up the phone, to see who is calling and it reads "T". Sheila wondered to herself to say… "Who's T?" So, looking back at Roderick, passed out still, she takes his phone with her to the master bedroom, to investigate the calls and messages he's been getting. She sits down at the edge of their bed to investigate the missing call and text messages that read "Where are you?" "Heads up!" "Why aren't you picking up?" "Call me asap!" Sheila now devastated, after reading all the texts, including sexual gestures, she became highly disturbed and even angrier to say… "How stupid I've been all this time!" "Why didn't I see this coming?" "All I ever did was be a faithful wife to him and this is how he repays me!"

Now overwhelmed in grief and bitter emotions, numbed in her mind and body from disbelief at the unexpected occurrences, she hears the phone ringing in her hand from the vibration of the phone she never let go… She looked down at the ID caller to find once again, its "T" she picked up the call and to begin to say something, but before she had a chance, the caller said… "I've been trying to call you all this morning, to see what time we're hooking up as you promised." "Hello!" "Say something!" Sheila now speechless, because the voice sounded familiar but wasn't exactly sure until… "Roderick, say something!" "What's wrong?" "Is your wife standing near you?" "Yes Trina, his wife is right here." "Sheila!" "I'm, I'm so sorry Girl!" Trina said. "I didn't mean for it to happen this way…" "Don't worry Trina, it won't happen again!" (Click!)

After Sheila hung up on Trina, she suddenly feels that she's about to lose it, finding out it was Trina all this time. Sheila says to herself… "What even hurts me more is that I got played by both Trina and my husband!" "Just wait until I get my hands on that hoe, but first my husband, the biggest hoe!" She went back to the guestroom, where Roderick still passed out from the beers he drank, Sheila reached into his pants pockets, to see if he had rubbers on him, in preparation to meet Trina, but none to be found. Sheila began to shake Roderick's whole body in attempt to wake him up, but to no avail. Now drenched in tears, to the point it was all over her face and hands, she went back into the master bedroom, to look, to see if he had condoms stashed in the dresser drawers, but to find something else. She stood back in amazement of her discovery with her left hand over her mouth and her right hand touching the object she discovered… "A gun Roderick? A gun?" "When was you going to tell me that you owned a gun?"

She turned over and looked at their wedding picture that was on their end table to ask… "How could you Roderick? Was you planning to kill me?" "I thought that you loved me! When was you going to tell me that you and Trina was seeing each other? After I was dead?" She said with tears. Feeling a breakdown coming on her, she quickly tried to shake it off by going back to the guest room where Roderick lied passed out still. Sheila propped herself on top of him and leaned over to him, gently rubbed his bald head, and caressed his face and cheeks to whisper… "Roderick wake up!" "Come on baby wake up!" She kissed his forehead and began to grope him in hopes he would wake up… "Come on baby, Mommy want some loving…" Sheila said. Roderick slowly begins to wake up to say "Hey what's up." "Hey baby come give it to me!" Sheila seductively suggested. "Whoa Sheila! What are you doing!!" Roderick shouted. "Quit playing Sheila!!" "Shut up Roderick! Shut up!" Roderick tried to get up, but Sheila had him pinned down while pointing the gun to his temple. "Stop Sheila I'm not playing!" He shouted. "Shut up Rod!" "It's over, you are busted!" "Wait, wait, what are you talking about?" He asked. "It's over Rod!" "Wait, wait, let me talk!" "No baby, it's too late to talk." "You've been caught cheating on me with another woman or man, as you call it! Trina told me everything, and that you been sleeping with her!" "Naw, naw Sheila don't do it!!" "You've been busted Roderick, and it's now time to pay up!" "Wait!!!!!!!!!!!".…………..

3 shots fired.……………

1 Shot to Roderick's temple.…………..

1 Shot to Roderick's chest.……………..

1 shot to herself.………

"What we sow, we also reap!"